On the surface Jackie looked sweet, almost fragile....

But Wyatt had glimpsed the hard steel beneath that soft exterior. A bodyguard. Who would've thought it?

"So tell me about the dead man," she said.

"I didn't kill him."

"Didn't say you did."

He pointed to a dirt road up ahead. "Take a left."

Jackie turned, her gaze straying to the rearview. "We're being followed."

He might think the woman was paranoid or crazy. But considering this morning he'd found a dead body on his porch and spent the past seven hours in jail, he wasn't going to doubt her. Sticking his head out the window, he strained to listen. "A motorcycle."

"Hang on!" She stomped on the brake and twisted the wheel, sending the truck into a spin and coming to a halt facing the way they'd come. Their headlights swept over an oncoming motorcycle...moving at a good clip and heading straight for them.

Books by Terri Reed

Love Inspired Suspense

Love Inspired

TERRI REED

At an early age Terri Reed discovered the wonderful world of fiction and declared she would one day write a book. Now she is fulfilling that dream and enjoys writing for Love Inspired Books. Her second book, *A Sheltering Love,* was a 2006 RITA® Award finalist and a 2005 National Readers' Choice Award finalist. Her book *Strictly Confidential,* book five in the Faith at the Crossroads continuity series, took third place in the 2007 American Christian Fiction Writers Book of the Year Award, and *Her Christmas Protector* took third place in 2008. She is an active member of both Romance Writers of America and American Christian Fiction Writers. She resides in the Pacific Northwest with her college-sweetheart husband, two wonderful children and an array of critters. When not writing, she enjoys spending time with her family and friends, gardening and playing with her dogs.

You can write to Terri at P.O. Box 19555 Portland, OR 97280. Visit her on the web at www.loveinspiredauthors.com, leave comments on her blog, www.ladiesofsuspense.blogspot.com, or email her at terrireed@sterling.net.

THE COWBOY TARGET

Terri Reed

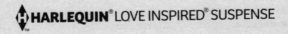

HARLEQUIN® LOVE INSPIRED® SUSPENSE

Recycling programs for this product may not exist in your area.

 ™ LOVE INSPIRED BOOKS

ISBN-13: 978-0-373-44529-5

THE COWBOY TARGET

www.LoveInspiredBooks.com

Printed in U.S.A.

But Jesus called the children to him and said,
"Let the little children come to me,
and do not hinder them, for the kingdom of God
belongs to such as these. I tell you the truth,
anyone who will not receive the kingdom of God
like a little child will never enter it."
—*Luke* 18:16,17

To my children—you are the joys of my life.

ONE

There was a dead man on his porch.

Wyatt Monroe looked into the man's beaten face. Dried blood covered his body in dark splotches. Purple bruises mottled his skin. Lifeless eyes stared back at Wyatt.

Recognition rocked him back on his heels.

He grabbed his cell from his back pocket and dialed 911. His gaze scanned the buildings of his ranch—his foreman's house, the hay barn and stables, the equipment shed, feed shed—and the Wyoming landscape beyond, searching for the threat. Snow swirled in the air and covered the pastureland spread out over the sixty-thousand-acre ranch.

All appeared quiet and undisturbed on this brisk March morning.

"Lane County Emergency Department," the female operator answered. "What's your emergency?"

"Eleanor, this is Wyatt Monroe."

"Hey, Wyatt. What's wrong?"

He could picture the older woman who'd been manning the town's emergency line for longer than he could remember. But that was life in Lane County, Wyoming.

Predictable and steady. The way he wanted his life to be. Sans dead bodies.

"Is Gabby okay?"

The concern in Eleanor's voice wrapped around Wyatt and squeezed. Too many people in this town wondered if his little girl was safe with him. Three years after his wife, Dina, had died, he couldn't escape the speculation and suspicion. Even from her grave she was wreaking havoc with his life.

That was what women did. They wormed their way into a guy's heart and then stomped all over it. His mother had done it to his father. Dina had done it to Wyatt.

Never again.

His gaze lifted to the second floor of his family home. The dormer window with the pink, frilly curtains was closed to protect his four-year-old from the winter weather.

But how protected could she be if someone had dumped a body on his front porch so callously?

"Gabby's fine," he said, assuring himself as much as Eleanor. "It's George Herman."

Eleanor snorted. "What's that rascal gone and done now?"

Wyatt's gaze strayed back to the bloodied, lifeless body of his ranch hand. Gaping wounds littered his torso. Bruises covered his face. The skin of his knuckles had been scraped raw. Poor George.

It was no secret Wyatt and George hadn't seen eye to eye on most things. But the man had been a hand on the Monroe Ranch since Wyatt had been old enough to sit a horse. Wyatt couldn't bring himself to fire him.

He and Dad had been friends. And George didn't have anyone or anyplace else to go.

"Got himself killed." A shudder worked through him. He worked to keep his voice calm. "I found him on my front porch."

Death was a part of life. He knew that. He'd dealt with more than his share. But still...

The silence on the line was as loud as a shotgun blast.

Wyatt swallowed back the memories of the last time he'd had to make an emergency call. The night Dina had died. The night the town had turned on him, accusing him of murder.

A burn spread through his belly. Her death had been an accident. But few believed him. Including his own mother. Which solidified his belief that women couldn't be trusted with his heart.

"I'll inform the sheriff," Eleanor stated with a decidedly cool tone to her voice.

"Appreciate it," he said and hung up.

The front door opened behind him with a barely discernible squeak. Wyatt pivoted and strode toward Gabby, her sweet, freckled face peering through the crack in the doorway.

"Daddy?"

He shooed her back inside with a wave of his hands. "It's too cold for you to come outside in your jammies." He stepped inside the warm house and firmly shut the door behind him. His daughter didn't need to see the horror on the porch.

Gabby lifted her arms. "I want pancakes."

"When Penny comes over, I'm sure she'll make you some pancakes—if you ask politely." He glanced at the clock. His pulse still thundered like the horses he bred. Penny would be here any minute. His foreman's wife watched Gabby during the day while Wyatt worked.

Swinging Gabby into his arms, he carried her into the living room and deposited her on the worn brown leather couch. "For now, why don't you snuggle up under this blanket?" He tucked a fussy blue blanket around her tiny body. "As a special treat today, you can watch some TV before breakfast."

Her bright green eyes lit up. "Barney!"

The favorite of every preschooler. He kissed the top of her curly red head before turning on the television and tuning into the channel with the big purple dinosaur. "Gabby, I need you to stay right here, okay?"

She didn't answer. Her attention remained captivated by the singing character on the screen.

Love for this little child pierced his heart. He searched her sweet face. She looked so much like Dina, the same red hair, the same freckled nose and emerald eyes. He didn't see any of himself in Gabby. Like a knife, the thought sliced as deeply as it always did when he let his mind travel down that perilous road.

A scream from outside split the air. Wyatt flinched. Penny had arrived. He'd hoped to get back out front before she'd walked over. One last glance at Gabby assured him she was too engrossed in her show to have heard the scream. He hurried out the front door.

Penny Kirk clutched a hand over her mouth and held on to the porch railing with the other. Beneath the bright red wool cap pulled low over her graying hair, her lined face was pale, her eyes wide with shock.

Grimly stepping over George, Wyatt went to Penny

and steered her away from the sight of the dead man. Her scream had brought others pouring out of the outer buildings.

Penny's husband, Carl, ran to his wife's side. His untucked plaid shirt flapped against his denim-clad thighs, and white shaving foam covered half of his face. "What happened? Are you hurt?" He wrapped his arm around Penny.

"George," she said and broke into tears.

Wyatt met Carl's gaze. Gesturing with his head, he announced, "He's dead. On the porch."

Carl's gaze widened. Wyatt saw the questions, the suspicions, and knew this was just the beginning of what promised to be a mess.

Wyatt recaptured Penny's gaze. "Gabby's inside watching TV."

Penny's eyes filled with horror. "Did she...?"

Wyatt shook his head. Thankful for that.

Penny blew out a breath of relief. "I'll go to her."

Grateful to the older couple who'd virtually adopted him and Gabby as family, Wyatt knew he and Gabby wouldn't have fared well without them over the years. They'd come on board the ranch before Wyatt's dad passed on, had witnessed the turmoil of Wyatt's marriage and had stepped in as surrogate grandparents for Gabby as soon as she was born. Dina had resisted their help, but Wyatt thanked God for them every day.

The sound of tires coming up the snow-packed gravel drive drew Wyatt's attention. The sheriff's brown sedan pulled to a stop. Two deputy cars and the medical examiner's van pulled in behind him.

Wyatt went to meet the law officer, who was climbing out of his vehicle.

Sheriff Craig Landers was tall and broad shouldered beneath his brown leather jacket and tan uniform. His salt-and-pepper hair poked out from the curled edges of a tan Stetson. His sharp gray eyes took in everything. The crowd of ranch hands circling the front porch, the body lying at the top of the stairs. And Wyatt.

Forcing himself to stand taller, Wyatt met his stepfather's gaze head-on.

"Wyatt."

"Sheriff."

The older man's eyes narrowed. "Give me the lowdown."

"I came out front about twenty minutes ago and found George just as he is."

"You didn't move the body, did you?"

"No." Wyatt had learned the hard way that contaminating a crime scene would only make him look guilty. At least, it had with Dina. He'd tried to give her CPR. Her blood had ended up on his clothes. For some, that was enough to label him responsible for her death.

Thankfully, Wyatt had God and a lack of incriminating evidence on his side. He could only hope and pray God would see him through this ordeal, too.

"Good." Landers strode forward. "Okay, everyone back away. Let Andrew through," he said, indicating the medical examiner.

Wyatt watched as Andrew, an older man with a full beard and wire-rimmed glasses, examined the body.

George had been ornery and arrogant, but he didn't

deserve to die. Who would do this? And why leave him on Wyatt's porch?

"Wyatt, you understand we have to search the grounds." Landers's voice broke through his thoughts. The sheriff's voice held a note of compassion.

"Knock yourself out," Wyatt stated. He didn't have anything to hide. And he intended to be right on their heels doing a search of his own. Nobody harmed one of his people. "Tell your boys to be mindful of Gabby. She's in the living room watching television."

"Sheriff!"

Wyatt turned toward where a deputy stood beside the open door to Wyatt's dark blue truck. Winter sunlight glinted off the object the deputy held up with a gloved hand.

The air left Wyatt's lungs in a rush.

His steel-bladed hunting knife, covered in blood.

Jackie Blain punched the freestanding, heavy black bag. Jab, jab with the right hand. *Whack* with her left elbow. Right foot roundhouse kick. Jab, jab. *Whack*. Kick. She focused on the punching bag with single-minded attention. For the moment, she was in the heat of battle against an imaginary assailant wanting to part her from her client. Not happening on her watch. Ever. That was why she trained two to three hours a day. At least, every day that she wasn't on an assignment.

The trilling sound of her cell phone broke through her concentration. Giving the bag one last jab, she whirled away and jumped over her sleeping English bulldog, Spencer, to grab the phone off the island counter.

"Blain," she answered.

"Jackie, it's your uncle Carl," the voice on the other end said in her ear.

Taken by surprise, she smiled. Carl was her mother's older brother. "Hey. Wow, long time no hear."

She picked up a white terry-cloth towel from the pile sitting atop the bar stool and wiped her face and neck.

"The street runs both ways, young lady," her uncle chided.

"Yeah, I know. Sorry 'bout that. I did call at Christmas and left a message."

"I know. And we were remiss in not returning the call."

She shrugged away his comment and turned to stare at the present they'd sent, an eleven-by-eleven landscape painted by a local Wyoming artist, which hung on her kitchen wall. The gift canceled out not returning her call.

Walking to the window of her apartment located in Boston's Back Bay neighborhood, Jackie pushed the blinds apart with her free hand. A fresh layer of snow covered the street below. Beyond the roofline of the apartments across the street, the downtown Boston skyline glistened in the midmorning winter sun. She never tired of looking at the city. So different from the flat cornfields of Iowa where she'd grown up. "So, how are you? Have you heard from my parents?"

"We're okay," he said, but something in his tone didn't ring true with his words.

She dropped the blinds back in place. Her heart sped up. Her breath lay trapped beneath her ribs. She hadn't heard from her parents in a couple of weeks. They were on a cruise in the Mediterranean. "And Mom and Dad?"

"They're good as far as I know," he quickly assured her.

Tension left her body in a rush of relief. "But something's wrong."

"Yes. We could sure use your help," Carl said.

She blinked. Her uncle and aunt had never asked for anything from her before. This must be serious. "Sure. What do you need?"

"It's Wyatt Monroe. He needs you."

Sinking into the reclining leather love seat, her one piece of furniture that hadn't come from a secondhand store, she asked, "Your employer? Needs me?"

She'd never met Mr. Monroe. In fact, she'd never visited Wyoming, where her uncle and aunt lived. She'd thought about it back when her life had turned upside down. But then she'd found Trent Associates and, well, she never got around to making the trip that far west. She'd returned home to Atkins, Iowa, a couple of times, but preferred her parents to come to Boston. Going back to her hometown only stirred up old anger and humiliation. And reinforced the painful lessons she'd learned about love. Never fall for someone you work with. And never, ever give anyone that much power over your heart.

She shuddered and pushed away the memories threatening to surface. She had a good job now with Trent Associates as a protection specialist. She had a place to belong. She had coworkers who respected her, cared for her and made her feel connected. Protecting others was what she was good at. And she had her dog, Spencer, for company. That was all she needed.

"Wyatt's in trouble." Carl's words broke through her

thoughts. "Someone's framing him for the murder of one of his ranch hands."

That piqued her interest. And raised her skepticism. Four years as a deputy sheriff did that to a person. "Are you sure he didn't do it?"

"I know he didn't." His voice was adamant.

Still, old habits of suspicion held firm. "Are you his alibi?"

After a moment's hesitation, he said, "No. He doesn't have one."

"Not good for him." She kicked off her cross-trainers with a sigh. Her feet cooled immediately. She'd worked up a sweat on this cold March morning. "I trust he has a good lawyer?"

"I've hired one. Against his wishes."

Jackie frowned. "Is his objection to *you* hiring the lawyer or to the *lawyer* himself?"

Carl heaved a beleaguered sigh. "Both. He's innocent and doesn't see why he needs a lawyer."

Either the man was overconfident in the justice system or not right in the head. Jackie figured it was probably a little of both. "What can I do to help?"

"Would you come here? Help us prove he's innocent?"

She sat back. "Uncle Carl, I'm not in law enforcement anymore. I'm sure the police there will do a thorough investigation."

"Maybe. But I'd feel better if you'd come out and keep an eye on the investigation. There are complications."

"What kind of complications? Either he did the deed, or he didn't. The evidence will prove it one way or another."

"It's not that simple here. Wyatt has a past," Carl said.

Jackie wrinkled her nose. "We all have a past, Uncle Carl. That won't affect the evidence."

"What if someone wanted it to?"

Her mind jumped back to Carl's earlier statement. "You really think someone is trying to frame him?"

"I do." He lowered his voice. "Plus, there's bad blood between the sheriff and Wyatt that goes back a long ways."

Not a mess she wanted to get involved in.

"I have a job here. A good job." Even as the words left her mouth, she knew she was overdue to take some vacation time. Her boss, James, had gone so far as to tell her if she didn't take some R & R by spring, he'd bench her for a few weeks to give her some forced downtime.

"Then I'll hire you if that's what it takes," Carl said with a flinty edge.

He wasn't going to let this go. "This means a lot to you, doesn't it?"

"Helping Wyatt means everything to Penny and me." Carl cleared his throat. "You know we wouldn't ask if it weren't important. If Wyatt is convicted of this crime… We can't let it happen. Gabby needs her father."

"I take it Gabby's his daughter?" Jackie remembered her mother mentioning that Mr. Monroe was a widower with a child.

"Yep. A four-year-old bundle of joy. We're very attached to Wyatt and Gabby. He's like a son to us," he said, his voice thick with emotion. "Gabby's like a granddaughter."

Sympathy and understanding twisted her up inside. Her aunt and uncle had tried for a child for many years

but never conceived. Jackie had often wondered why
God had never answered their prayers for a child. But
apparently He had a plan. Which evidently included
Wyatt and Gabby Monroe.

Now the man her aunt and uncle claimed as their surrogate son was in trouble. And they were asking her for
help. How could she refuse?

A chill chased down her spine. It had to be her body's
core temperature lowering. Certainly not some warning of doom.

"I'll come as soon as I can."

"Thank you."

The relief in his words wrapped around her like duct
tape. "Uncle Carl, I don't know that I'll be able to do
much other than make sure everything is done by the
book."

"I understand."

She hoped so. She'd hate for them to have high expectations that she couldn't meet.

After hanging up, she sat down on the floor next to
Spencer and rubbed the dog behind the ears. "Okay, boy.
Looks like we're taking a trip to Wyoming."

TWO

As darkness descended, Wyatt's jail cell became gloomier, if that were even possible. He sat on the hard bench that served as bed and sofa—the only furniture allowed in the Lane County jail.

The door to the cell rattled as a deputy inserted the key into the lock and swung the metal cage door open. "Wyatt, you've got visitors."

"Who?" Wyatt asked.

"Lawyers, I guess," Deputy Rawlings replied.

Wyatt scrubbed a hand over his face, and the bristles of his beard scraped his palm. His eyes were gritty, and his body ached from the uncomfortable bench. He'd told Carl not to bother with a lawyer. Wyatt would pay the bail and do his own investigation. He knew how a criminal investigation would go in this town. Been there, done that. He'd have to prove his innocence himself. Finding the knife in his possession looked bad, but that wasn't proof he'd killed George. They couldn't know if the blood on the knife belonged to George yet. Not until they did a DNA test. And he knew that would take weeks, if not longer.

Wyatt heaved himself to his feet, picked up his Stetson and plopped it on his head. At six feet four inches, he had to duck slightly to walk out of the cell, or he'd bump his head and knock his hat off on the metal door frame. He followed Rawlings to an interrogation room. The same one he'd spent several hours in while the sheriff grilled him about George and the murder.

Now the room was filled not only with the sheriff, but also the town's newest attorney. Bruce Kelly sat at the table with a file folder laid out in front of him. He wore a pin-striped suit and sported thick black-framed glasses. His brown hair was parted in the middle and slicked back.

Wyatt had never had an occasion to deal with Mr. Kelly, a city slicker lured to this part of the country by a local gal. Kelly had opened up shop two years ago. Wyatt doubted he'd ever defended an accused murderer before.

But it was the petite woman standing next to the table and arguing with the sheriff who grabbed Wyatt's attention by the throat and trapped his breath in his chest. She hadn't seemed to notice he'd entered the room, which gave him a moment to inspect her. He didn't know her, but he sure liked what he saw.

Not more than five feet five inches tall with a head of wild blond curls held back by a clawlike clip, she was dressed in formfitting blue jeans, tall brown leather boots and a red leather jacket. She planted her small, dainty fists on her slim hips and managed to stare down her pert nose at the much taller sheriff. A feat Wyatt wouldn't have thought possible, except he was witness to it.

Impressive. And gutsy.

"Your evidence is circumstantial at best," she declared in a honeyed voice.

Wyatt snorted. He was well aware of how circumstantial evidence could convict someone in the court of public opinion.

"That's true," Bruce Kelly interjected. The lawyer appeared a bit flummoxed, his gaze shifting between the fiery blonde and the intimidating sheriff.

"His prints are on the knife," Landers countered, keeping his attention on the woman.

"Understandable since it's his knife," she shot back. "There are also textured prints from a glove."

"Which he could have been wearing," Landers said, darting a glance at Wyatt.

Wyatt could see the irritation in Landers's eyes and couldn't help feeling a little jolt of satisfaction. It was good to see someone else getting Landers's goat for once. Growing up, Wyatt had only ever received grief from his stepfather. Still did, if truth be told.

Without so much as glancing in his direction, the woman tucked in her chin. "Really? So you honestly think he's gonna go to the trouble of killing the guy, remove his body from the primary crime scene, dump him on his own porch for all the world to see, then be dumb enough to leave the knife in plain sight but ditch the gloves? Not likely. This has all the earmarks of a setup, and if you can't see that…"

"Careful, Ms. Blain," Landers warned with a glower. "I agree there is more going on here than meets the eye."

She smirked. Wyatt held back a grin.

Landers met Wyatt's gaze. "You're free to go, Wyatt. Just don't leave town."

As if Wyatt would. Where would he go? This was his home. Gabby was here. But he refrained from responding. Instead he met the bright blue-eyed gaze of his mysterious defender. She stared back with unabashed curiosity. He didn't know this woman, so why would she defend him? Was she the lawyer Carl Kirk said he was hiring? But then why was Bruce Kelly here?

Bruce cleared his throat and rose to his feet. "Now that we have that settled, I'll speak to my client alone."

His client?

Sheriff Landers gave a curt nod and exited the room.

Wyatt crossed his arms over his chest. "So which one of you is my lawyer?"

Jackie couldn't help but appreciate the hunk standing before her. She'd never really been into the cowboy type, but this one...whew, sure made a girl's heart beat faster.

Tall and lean, he was dressed in worn denim with a soft-looking chambray shirt stretched over shoulders that made her think he could support the whole state of Wyoming on his back. He had a ruggedly handsome face with a firm jaw and dark, intense eyes beneath a well-loved traditional cowboy hat. In the dim light of the interrogation room, she couldn't tell if his hair was black or dark brown. She guessed she'd have to wait for the light of day to find out.

A little thrill zoomed through her tummy at the prospect of spending time with such an attractive man.

So not a good reaction to be having. Wyatt Monroe could be a murderer.

"*I* am," Bruce said. "Carl Kirk asked me to represent you."

Wyatt's gaze flicked over the lawyer before settling once again on Jackie. Curiosity and something else she couldn't decipher shone in the inky depths of his eyes. "And you are?"

She stepped forward and thrust out her hand. "Jackie Blain. Carl and Penny Kirk are my uncle and aunt."

He stared at her outstretched hand for a moment as if she were offering him a stick of dynamite. She waited, not about to let this cowboy think for a moment that he intimidated her with his brooding attitude.

Slowly he unfolded his arms and grasped her hand in his much bigger one. Their palms met. Warmth spread up her arm and settled beneath her breastbone.

"Ms. Blain, why are you here?" he asked as he quickly let go of her hand.

She flexed her fingers and jammed her hands in the pockets of her jacket. "I have a background in law enforcement, and Uncle Carl asked if I'd come out and see what I could do to help."

He took a moment to absorb that before saying, "Well, you've done your good deed for the day." He tipped his hat. "I appreciate it. Sorry you had to come all the way from…"

"Boston."

His eyebrows rose. "Boston. Well, don't let me keep you. I'm sure you're anxious to get back to the city."

She nearly laughed but settled for a grin. "Oh, you're not getting rid of me that easily, cowboy. I'm your ride back to the ranch."

His jaw firmed in clear displeasure.

Jackie turned to Mr. Kelly. "Is there anything else you require at the moment?"

The bemused expression on the man's face was comical. "No. Unless Mr. Monroe has some questions for me."

Wyatt shook his head. "I didn't kill George."

"Then there shouldn't be any problems. I'll let you both know—" he shifted his gaze to Jackie and then back to Wyatt "—if there are any developments."

"Good deal," Jackie said and headed for the door, aware of Wyatt's scowl. "Come along, cowboy. I'm hungry, and Aunt Penny's made meat loaf."

Wyatt ground his back teeth as the new arrival in his already tangled life sashayed toward the jail door. Who did this lady think she was, anyway? It was one thing for her to go toe-to-toe with Landers—he rather liked that—but he wasn't used to being ordered around. Especially by a diminutive spitfire with big blue eyes and a pert nose.

The Kirks' niece. She'd never been out to the ranch before. Made sense if she lived in Boston. Boston! How had she arrived so quickly? He'd been taken into custody this morning. It would take at least eight hours to fly from Boston because there were no direct flights between the cities and another two hours of driving from Laramie, yet she looked as fresh as a daisy on a spring day.

Carl shouldn't be sticking his nose where it didn't belong.

After retrieving his personal belongings, Wyatt lengthened his stride to keep up with Jackie as she left the sheriff's station and headed to the parking lot toward a big black SUV.

"Hold up," he said, snagging her by the elbow. She tensed beneath his hand. "When did you get in?"

"We flew in around four. Rented this baby and drove over from Laramie."

"Who's we?"

"Spencer." She tugged her elbow free and opened the driver's side door. "Hey, boy. Miss me?"

Wyatt peered over her shoulder into the vehicle. A white-and-brown bulldog sat on the passenger seat, his tongue hanging out and his brown eyes staring at Jackie with devotion. He let out a single woof.

Wyatt blinked. "You brought your *dog?*"

She climbed in and started the engine. "I wouldn't *leave* him." She gave him a pointed look.

"I thought snub-nosed dogs weren't allowed on commercial airlines," he said.

"Some don't. We flew over on the Trent plane."

"Trent? What's that?"

"Trent Associates. Private protection specialists." She grinned. "At your service."

No wonder she didn't look travel weary and had arrived so quickly. A company plane. Impressive. He wondered what she did for Trent Associates. He tried to remember if Carl had ever said. Probably some sort of admin job, like his mother. Marsha Landers was the administrative assistant to the mayor.

"If you're coming, you better get in." With that, Jackie shut the door.

For a moment he stood there in stunned silence. He'd never met anyone like this woman. On the surface she looked sweet and almost fragile with her small stature and delicate features, but he'd glimpsed the hard steel beneath that soft exterior when she stood up to his step-father, the sheriff.

That earned her points in his book. Just as long as she didn't get too used to bossing him around.

He opened the passenger door and eyed the dog, who stared back impassively at him. "I'm not riding in back."

The mutt looked friendly enough, but Wyatt wasn't taking any chances. He kept his hands far away from the drooling canine's mouth. That jaw looked pretty strong.

Jackie whistled softly and pointed her finger toward the floor. The dog hopped down between the captain's seats. Wyatt settled into the passenger seat and barely had his seat belt buckled before she took off, her foot a heavy weight on the accelerator.

"Whoa, there is a speed limit," he said.

She eased up on the gas. "Sorry. Force of habit. Driving aggressively is part of my job."

Curious, Wyatt studied her profile. There was just the slightest hint of freckles across her cheeks. She had a nice jawline and a slender neck. Delicate, even. "And what job would that be?"

"I work for Trent Associates. We're a protection specialist agency."

"You said that. But what do *you* do?"

The droll glance she sent his way made him feel as if he'd just said the Grand Tetons were molehills. "Protection."

He tucked in his chin. "Protection? As in body-guard?"

"Yep."

He couldn't picture this itty-bitty woman protecting anyone. A smile tugged at his lips. "Let me get this straight—you're a bodyguard?"

She sighed. "I know. Difficult to believe, right?"

"You could say that."

"I get that a lot. At first." She slid another speculative glance his way. "What were you thinking I did for a living?"

He eyed her authoritative grasp on the steering wheel and amended his earlier assumption. "I'd have guessed schoolteacher, or principal, even."

She laughed. "No. But I do like kids."

A leaden weight settled on Wyatt's heart, and he turned to watch the Wyoming sky out the passenger window. Images of his daughter floated through his mind. The day she'd taken her first steps, the night she'd split her lip on the coffee table, her delight when she opened her Christmas presents. His heart ached that Gabby would grow up without a mother.

As they reached the outskirts of town, Jackie pointed to the computer display on the dashboard. "You can put your address in the GPS system."

He shook his head. "That would take you the long way around. We'll go a more direct route. I'll tell you when to turn."

"Suit yourself. So, tell me about George Herman."

The image of George's battered face came to mind with a fair dose of horror and regret. Had he said "good job" to George lately?

Wyatt ran a hand over his face. "Not much to tell. My dad hired him as a ranch hand about twenty years ago. He was a hard worker when he wanted to be. Had strong opinions about most things and a penchant for fighting."

Her eyebrows rose. "Ever with you?"

"We've had our share of arguments over the years. He didn't think I was running the ranch the way I ought to."

"Any of these arguments turn physical?"

He slanted her a sharp glance. She sounded just like his stepfather in interrogation mode. "Why would you ask that?"

"Prior history always plays a part in a case like this. Establishes a pattern. Motive. You two could have been arguing and it turned physical. His death could have been an accident." She looked at the road, then casually met his gaze. "Do you drink, Mr. Monroe?"

"No, I don't drink. And I didn't kill him." Why did everyone want to believe he did?

"I didn't say you did. Just pointing out one theory."

"I'd rather you didn't." He pointed to a dirt road up ahead on the left. "Just past the mailboxes, take a left."

She took the turn. The vehicle's headlights cut through the darkness, illuminating the snow-covered dirt road. "Okay. Then who else wanted him dead? Did he have any enemies? Threats made to his life?"

"I don't know." He'd thought about that while he'd sat in the jail cell. George wasn't the most congenial of souls, but Wyatt couldn't think of anyone on the ranch or in town who'd want to hurt him. "He didn't confide in me. I don't know if he'd been threatened or felt that he was in danger. We weren't close."

She fell silent as she drove. Wyatt watched the world outside the vehicle pass by. He didn't need daylight to know every inch of his family spread, to see the yawning expanse of flatland stretching off to the left of the road. To the right, the distant outline of the Snowy Range

Mountains reaching toward the heavens was barely visible against the night sky.

"Does this road get much traffic?" she asked, her gaze straying to the rearview mirror.

He shook his head. "No. Only goes to the house. Why?"

"We're being followed."

He twisted around in the seat. Behind them lay only darkness. "I don't see anything."

"It's there. I caught a glimpse of moonlight reflecting off chrome."

If someone hadn't just tried to frame him for murder, he'd think the woman driving the SUV was paranoid or crazy. Or both. But considering that this morning he'd found a dead body on his porch and had spent the past several hours in jail being grilled like rainbow trout on the barbecue, he wasn't going to doubt her.

If she said something was behind them, he believed her. Still, he couldn't see anything.

He powered down the window. Cold air swirled through the cab of the SUV. The sound of the rig's tires crunching over the packed snow and dirt nearly masked an out-of-place noise. The rev of an engine. But not from a car or truck.

Sticking his head out the window, he strained to listen, to discern what it was he heard.

"A motorcycle," he decided and rolled the window back up.

"Anyone at the ranch have a motorcycle?"

"No. Not that I know of."

"Are you buckled in?" Jackie asked.

Reflexively, he touched the buckle to assure himself he was indeed strapped in securely. "Yes."

"Hang on to Spencer."

He reached down and grabbed the dog by the collar as she stomped on the brake and twisted the wheel, sending the big, lumbering SUV into a spin and coming to a halt facing the way they'd come. The SUV's headlights swept over an oncoming motorcycle. The driver swerved at the last second and drove past them, barely avoiding becoming a hood ornament. The single rider wore all black. The machine he rode was also black, except for chrome exhaust pipes.

The motorcycle roared down the road toward the ranch and disappeared.

Jackie made a three-point turn then punched the gas, chasing after the motorcycle. But he was already too far ahead for the headlights to find him in the dark. The tracks glistened in the beam of light. So did the gently falling snow.

Anxiety tripped down Wyatt's spine. What if the rider reached the house before they did? What would he do? Was the motorcyclist the one who'd killed George and framed Wyatt?

Jackie kept the gas floored, expertly controlling the speeding vehicle on the slick, snow-packed road. There was more than met the eye in this petite package. He added *competent driver* to his list of her attributes.

Two miles from the ranch, the cycle's tracks went off-road and disappeared into the dark.

"What's out there?" She slowed the vehicle to a stop.

"Cattle. That's the heifer pasture. There's a feed shed about two miles out. But there's a fence about a half mile from this road. The gate's on the other side of the pasture."

"Have you checked that fence lately?"

Wyatt took in a sharp breath. "That was George's job."

She tapped a finger on the steering wheel. "Maybe it's a squatter. Maybe George discovered him. Maybe that's why he was killed."

"That's a lot of maybes," Wyatt said, not liking the idea of someone trespassing on his land. "But if that theory were true, how'd the killer get my hunting knife, and why put George on my porch?"

"There's the rub. Where do you keep the knife?"

"In the truck, beneath the seat." Exactly where they'd found it. He didn't miss the slight narrowing of her eyes.

"Lot of people know you keep it there?"

"It wasn't a secret. And the truck's always in plain view."

Snow fell in earnest, a blanket of white that not even the headlights could cut through. That motorcycle rider wouldn't be getting very far in this blizzard.

"You lock the truck up at night?" Jackie asked.

A sinking feeling hit the pit of his stomach. "No. I don't."

She started the vehicle moving again. The windshield wipers worked hard to push the snow from the glass. "So in the middle of the night, anyone could have sneaked onto the ranch and taken it."

A sense of dread assailed him. "Just like they snuck onto the ranch and left George's body on my porch."

She slanted him a quick glance. "Exactly."

Which meant he and Gabby weren't safe.

THREE

"Once we get to the house and everyone is inside and buttoned down tight, I'll come back and have a look-see," Jackie stated.

"Not in this weather," Wyatt countered. A greenhorn like her would get herself lost in a whiteout like this. He wouldn't even chance it without careful preparation.

When they arrived at the house, the whole place was lit up. Carl, Penny and Gabby rushed outside onto the porch to greet them as they climbed out of the vehicle.

Relieved to know his family was okay, Wyatt let out the breath lodged beneath his ribs.

"Daddy!" his daughter squealed, barreling into his legs in a blur of fuzzy pink footsie jammies the second he stepped onto the porch.

"Hey, sweetie." Swamped with love for his little girl, he lifted her up so she could wrap her little arms around his neck. He tugged the corners of his jacket around her tiny body. His daughter loved him unconditionally. It should be enough. But Dina's words taunted him. Left a bitter taste in his mouth.

Carl and Penny hugged their niece.

Gabby pointed a finger at Jackie. "Who's that?"

With her arm around Jackie's waist, Penny said, "This is Jackie. Remember I told you we had a guest coming?"

Jackie smiled at Gabby. Wyatt liked the way Jackie's eyes softened when she looked at his daughter.

"Hi, there," Jackie said. Snowflakes balanced on her blond curls glistened in the glow of the porch light. "I love your freckles."

"Hi." Gabby returned the smile and ducked her head into Wyatt's neck. Her cold little nose pressed against his skin.

"You want to see something neat?" Jackie asked.

Gabby lifted her head and nodded.

Jackie hurried back to the vehicle. Carl followed. While he went to the back of the SUV, Jackie opened the passenger door. She lifted Spencer off the floor and carried him to the house.

Gabby nearly jumped out of Wyatt's arms. "Doggy."

He let her down so she could pet the canine.

Jackie's blue eyes twinkled as she squatted with the dog in her arms. "His name's Spencer. He's an English bulldog."

Gabby squealed with delight.

Carl hefted a big black duffel bag out of the back of the SUV and carried it to the smaller house across the driveway.

"You're both invited over for some meat loaf. It's Jackie's favorite," Penny said.

"Come on, sweetie. Let's go wash up." Wyatt took Gabby by the hand and watched Penny lead her niece to the small house across the drive from the main house.

Spencer trotted along behind them, leaving paw prints in the powdered snow.

As Wyatt led Gabby inside, she said, "I want a Spencer."

He wasn't surprised. He had a feeling there were many changes coming thanks to a certain blond guest.

And he wasn't sure they were all going to be good.

He took one last glance out at the snowy night before closing the door and prayed that tomorrow would be a better day. With no dead bodies.

The next morning Jackie was up and out for a recon run by 6:00 am. The blizzard had calmed, and the morning sun gleamed on a fresh layer of snow. Thankfully, she'd heard enough about Wyoming winters from her aunt and uncle that she'd packed appropriate clothing for a winter run.

Unfamiliar with the terrain, she'd opted to stay on the dirt road she'd driven last night. Though a good two inches of new powder covered the road, she didn't have any trouble discerning the path.

The magnificent landscape reminded her of a painting. The dark had hidden the blanket of white stretching out as far as the eye could see, broken only by the occasional copse of trees or outcropping of rocks. Off in the distance, majestic mountains rose like fingers pointing skyward, as if to remind her to look toward heaven.

Her breath puffed out in a small cloud in the frigid air. "Lord, thank You for the beauty all around me. Thank You for Your protection every day. Lord, I ask for Your guidance."

Because she didn't know what to make of Wyatt or

the situation. Someone tried to frame him for murder, but they'd done a sloppy job, which led her to believe it wasn't a very thought-out plan. Whoever was behind this wasn't organized and didn't really know what they were doing.

Was this some sort of personal vendetta against Wyatt? Or more of a spur-of-the-moment attempt by the killer to camouflage his identity? Was it someone on the ranch? Or could Wyatt have killed George and tried to make it look like a setup?

So many questions, but she had two weeks to figure it out. And she would. For her aunt and uncle. For that cute little freckled girl. And for the brooding, albeit handsome, rancher who seemed to carry the weight of the world on his wide shoulders.

When she'd left the house, she'd seen a couple of men already up and working in the barn and a few more in the big equipment shed. She'd taken a cursory look around. Asked a few questions of the hands. None had anything of use to tell her. None owned a motorcycle or knew of anyone who'd have been out the night before.

She'd asked Uncle Carl last night if he knew of anyone who owned a motorbike, but he didn't. She hadn't told them about the bike following them. She didn't want them to worry any more than they already were. She doubted anyone had slept well. She hadn't, which was another reason she'd needed the run. To clear the cobwebs from her brain.

At the four-mile mark on her pedometer, she turned around, heading back toward the ranch house. A shadow overhead grabbed her attention. She slowed her pace to watch a low-flying prop plane. She kept her eyes on the plane, noting that the aircraft flew in a grid pattern over the land. Back and forth, back and forth. She'd heard of cattle ranchers surveying their herds via the air. Maybe Wyatt had someone keeping watch over his cattle and horses from above.

She returned to the house to find Aunt Penny up and dressed. Spencer was waiting at the door. He sniffed her feet before losing interest and disappearing around the corner of the living room.

"You're up early," Penny said. "Would you like coffee?"

"Please."

"Do you run every day?"

"Most days." She sipped from the blue-and-white ceramic mug of steaming coffee Penny handed to her. "So what's the story with Wyatt and the sheriff? Uncle Carl said there's bad blood between them."

Penny pressed her lips together to form a tight line. "Sheriff Landers is Wyatt's stepfather."

"Ah." That explained why the sheriff had been both antagonistic yet reasonable. He could have easily pushed to keep Wyatt locked up until morning at least—or longer if he'd wanted to be a real pain. But he hadn't. Because of their family connection, no doubt. Though she'd sensed tension between them.

"Where is Wyatt's dad?"

"He passed on a decade ago."

A knock sounded at the kitchen door. Penny set her coffee in the sink before moving to answer the knock. Gabby and Wyatt stood on the threshold, bundled up for the walk across the driveway.

Gabby entered with an abundance of exuberance to

see Spencer. "Here, doggy, doggy. Spencer." She disappeared into the living room with Penny hot on her heels.

Wyatt gave Jackie an apologetic smile. "Hope you don't mind. She was dying to come see your dog."

"Not at all. Spencer will love the attention." She set her mug on the counter. "Can I get you a cup of coffee?"

"No, I've already had two cups." He eyed her running gear. "Exercising?"

"Running helps get me going in the morning."

"You came prepared."

"I did." She remembered what she'd seen on her run. "Do you have a plane surveying your cattle and horses?"

A scowl darkened his gaze. "No. But I know the one you're talking about. The white plane with the blue stripe. I've seen it occasionally. More so lately. Flies pretty low."

"That's it. If he's not flying on your behalf, I wonder what he's doing."

"Beats me. I can't control the airspace over the ranch."

"Worth checking on. There's gotta be some federal regulations about low-flying aircraft," she commented.

He shrugged. "Could be. I'll check into it. I've got work to do. Ranch won't run itself." With that, he tipped his hat and then headed toward the kitchen door.

"Wyatt."

He paused with his hand on the doorknob. "Yes?"

"Be careful. Make sure you're always with someone. Or two or three someones."

One dark eyebrow rose. "I can take care of myself."

Her mouth quirked. His ego was a bit touchy. She'd have to remember that. "I'm sure you can. But you don't want to leave yourself open to another frame job. Or, worst-case scenario, leave Gabby on her own."

Her meaning dawned in his dark eyes. "Right." He tipped his hat and walked out.

Every instinct told her to get up and follow him. As a bodyguard, her first priority was always to keep the protectee within reach. But he wasn't her protectee. He wasn't her client.

She'd come here with the promise to her aunt and uncle that she'd keep an eye on the investigation into who killed George Herman. Though thinking about who they were and why they'd tried to frame Wyatt for the murder burned in her veins like molten lava.

Her dormant investigative skills clamored to be put to work. They were skills she hadn't had to use often since leaving the Atkins County sheriff's department and going to work for Trent Associates as a protection specialist. Guarding people rarely required investigating murder.

She made her way to the living room and stopped in the arched doorway. Gabby sat on the floor with Spencer's head on her lap while Aunt Penny read her a story from a thick volume of children's classics. Seeing the child and dog so cozy made Jackie's heart twist in her chest. Her gaze moved to her aunt, to the contented expression on her lined face.

Jackie was glad God had brought this little girl into her aunt and uncle's life. Yearning gnawed at her as strong as hunger. Maybe someday God would give Jackie a little girl, too.

But first she would need a husband.

After her debacle with Jarrod, she wasn't sure she

was up to the task of looking for one. Finding a husband meant putting her heart on the line again. It would take a special man to coax her to venture toward marriage. As of yet, God hadn't brought such a man into her life. Maybe He never would.

Quietly she turned away from the touching sight and headed upstairs to shower and dress for the day.

An hour later, she headed outside dressed in thick wool cargo pants, a Dri-FIT T-shirt beneath a fleece pullover, a parka and insulated boots. She walked to the barn in search of Wyatt.

She came across her uncle in one of the stalls with a huge, beautiful black stallion. He pawed at the ground as Uncle Carl brushed his coat.

Leaning on the stall door, Jackie said, "He's gorgeous. What's his name?"

Carl smiled. "Alexander. He's a studhorse. We're getting him ready for a live cover in a few weeks."

"Do I want to know what that is?" she asked.

He laughed. "Making baby horses."

"Ah. Enough said." She glanced around. "Have you seen Wyatt?"

"May not be back from feeding the cattle."

The scuff of a boot on dirt alerted Jackie just as Wyatt said, "I'm right here."

Jackie turned around to find herself nose to chest with Wyatt. The scent of him, spicy and masculine, sent a shiver sliding over her. She tilted her head back. "Careful, cowboy. Sneaking up on me could get you hurt."

"I'll keep that in mind," he said with a slight twitch to his lips.

She planted her hand on his chest and applied pressure. She was more annoyed by her reaction to him than his closeness. "A little space, buckaroo, if you don't mind."

He grinned outright but stepped back. "You were looking for me?"

Trying to ignore how his devastating grin played havoc with her pulse, she strived for an authoritative tone. "I want you to take me to see where George Herman lived."

His grin evaporated. He gave her a curt nod. "What do you hope to find?"

"Something—anything—to indicate why he was killed."

"I'm sure the police have gone over the place with a fine-tooth comb."

"True, but they didn't have you along."

"I've already told you, we weren't close."

"No, but you knew the man for twenty years. Maybe you'll see something that seems normal to anyone else, but you know it is out of place for him."

His expression turned thoughtful. "Okay. Let's go. While we're out, we'll also check the feed shed."

Pleased by his proactiveness, she smiled. "Good idea."

"But I'm driving."

"Knock yourself out, cowboy." She followed him out of the barn to a dark blue 4x4 truck on steroids. Huge treaded tires, like ones on a tractor, dwarfed the body of the vehicle.

"You drive a monster truck?"

"When I need to get out on the land." He shrugged. "Besides, my regular rig is in police custody."

Right. The truck they'd found the incriminating knife in.

He came around to the passenger side and opened the door. "Need a lift?"

In her younger days, a remark such as that would have earned him a right jab or a stomp to his insole. Maturity had cooled her temper and allowed her to see the offer for what it was—politeness. "I can manage, thank you."

He held up his hands in mock surrender and took a half step back.

Thankfully, a bar jutted out of the side of the cab near the door. She reached up, barely managed to grab the bar, then swung one foot up to the running board, nearly doing the splits, and pulled herself up. Standing on the running board, she glanced back at Wyatt.

His lips twitched. "I'm duly impressed."

"You should be," she shot back and slid into the passenger seat. Good thing she stretched every day. That stunt could have seriously hurt.

He shut the door, came around to the driver's side and hefted himself up into the seat. The truck's engine rumbled like a pride of hungry lions.

"Do you enter this bad boy in monster-truck rallies or something?"

He scoffed. "No. Not my thing."

Somehow she didn't think so. Wyatt struck her as the homebody type. A man who liked his castle and didn't need to show off his testosterone to feel like a man. Not that she thought he was a wimp. There was strength in his hands, his arms. After her shower this morning, from her bedroom window, she'd watched him hefting hay bales from the back of a truck. The man was strong. Probably knew how to throw a punch, too.

But was he good with knives?

She'd give him the benefit of the doubt because she trusted her aunt and uncle implicitly. However, she would still need evidence. Her training wouldn't let her get away with less.

And so far that evidence pointed toward a setup.

But the question was, who was the mastermind? Someone out to get Wyatt? Or Wyatt trying to make it seem as if someone else was setting him up?

They drove to what looked like a small subdivision about ten minutes from the main house. "Are we still on your property?"

"Yes. These homes are leased to the ranch hands."

"You provide your hands with their own homes on your land?"

"I do. Keeps them close, and they have a place to call their own for as long as they work on the Monroe ranch."

"I'm impressed," she admitted.

He slid her a glance. "Thanks."

She popped open the door.

Putting a hand on her arm, he said, "Let me help you down, okay? Wouldn't want you to twist an ankle or something."

Heat from his touch penetrated the layers of clothes and seared her skin. "Uh, sure."

He climbed out, leaving behind a cold spot where his hand had been. Disconcerted by her reaction, she undid her seat belt, slid out onto the running board and waited for him to join her. He placed his hand on her waist. She settled her hands on his shoulders. Awareness shimmered over her, and attraction arced like a neon streak. She was surprised they weren't glowing.

He easily lifted her off the running board and slowly lowered her down to the ground. Her hands slid from his shoulders, down his arms, over the hard muscle of his biceps. When she had her balance, she nearly jumped away. Taking a steadying breath, she forced herself to tamp down the attraction.

The last thing she needed was to find herself with some sort of crush on this cowboy.

Better to concentrate on what they'd come to do so she could get back to her life without any damage to her heart or her pride.

At the front door, Wyatt removed a set of keys from his pocket and slid one into the lock. But the pressure of his hand pushed the unlatched door open.

Alarm bells went off in Jackie's head. She reached for her SIG hidden beneath her coat.

"The sheriff's people must not have closed the door all the way," Wyatt commented with a scowl.

Just as he moved to cross the threshold, she yanked him back. "Wait."

She inspected the door frame and the hinges.

"What are you looking for?" he asked.

"Explosives."

"Excuse me?"

"Welcome to my world."

He eyed her warily. "Seriously?"

Satisfied there weren't any trip wires, she said, "Never enter a questionable door without checking for a bomb. Too many targeted people have walked into a deadly blast."

Wyatt blinked and stared, his gaze bouncing between her face and the gun in her hand. "You really do this stuff for a living?"

She grinned. "Yep." She toed the door open and then entered, leading with her weapon.

"What in the world?" Wyatt said as he stepped in behind her.

The placed looked like a twister had recently touched down.

FOUR

Wyatt knew the mess he was seeing wasn't normal for George. Despite their differences, Wyatt had been inside George's house several times. The old man had been particular about having things orderly and neat. One of the many things George would get after Wyatt about. He didn't feel the ranch was as organized or run as efficiently as it could be.

But he never had a solution, only complaints.

Everything has a proper order, George would say. *If you don't honor that, you end up with nothing but chaos.*

Ironic that George's life should end in chaos. His place trashed, his body broken and his death a mystery. Didn't get much more chaotic than that. Regret slammed Wyatt again. George had been decent. But now it was too late to tell him that.

Jackie advanced, her weapon drawn. She opened a closet door, peered inside and then shut it. She moved down the hall and out of sight. A moment later she returned, her weapon out of sight. "No one here but us."

"Did the sheriff's people do this?" he asked, appalled at the idea that they'd destroy George's house.

"No way." Jackie set her hands on her hips. "This

place has been ransacked. The sheriff's department wouldn't have done this. And if the sheriff had found the house like this, there'd be crime-scene tape up." She shook her head. "This was done recently."

Meeting her gaze, he asked, "Motorcycle guy?"

"Hard to say."

He stared at the couch, its cushions ripped apart and the stuffing strewn all over. The coffee table had been dumped on its side. Books littered the floor in front of a bookcase that ran the length of the wall from carpet to ceiling. George had loved his books. The cover jacket of one caught his attention.

Stepping gingerly over a broken picture frame—an image of George with Wyatt's father, Emerson—he bent to pick up the book.

"Freeze!"

Startled by Jackie's barked command, he stilled, bent forward with his hand outstretched. His gaze shot to her. "What?"

She unzipped her parka to reveal a black waist pack. She unzipped the pack and withdrew two sets of disposable gloves, the kind you see in doctors' offices. She handed a pair to him. "Only touch the edges of anything. We don't want to leave any prints or smudge any viable ones."

Disconcerted, he took the gloves. "We should call Landers."

"We will, once we've had a chance to poke around."

"If there was something here worth finding that would lead to George's killer, don't you think the law and whoever did this would have found it?"

She lifted one shoulder in a shrug. "Maybe. Maybe not."

Shaking his head, he picked up the book, careful to touch only the edges of the faded gilt spine. The brushed-cloth cover was frayed at the edges, the pages inside yellowed. He opened the cover flap and read the inscription.

Emerson Stone Monroe, 1854

Wyatt's great-grandfather and his father's namesake.

This had been his father's favorite treasure. The volume he held in his hand was a first edition, American printing, worth some money. Wyatt hadn't seen the book since he was a kid. He'd wondered what happened to it. "Why did George have my father's book?"

"What's that?" Jackie asked. She'd moved to the desk in the corner and was methodically looking at every item on the surface and in the drawers.

"*Moby-Dick*. It was my father's at one time. Not sure why George had it."

"See, you found something odd that anyone else wouldn't have known was out of place. Maybe your dad gave it to him as a gift."

"Could be."

"Check it. Maybe George hid something in it."

Wyatt leafed through the pages and discovered an envelope addressed to George in Emerson Monroe's rigid lettering. Wyatt's heart squeezed tight. He knew what this was. Upon his father's death, Wyatt, Wyatt's mother, Carl and Penny Kirk, and George all received an envelope from Emerson. Wyatt's letter was tucked away in his top dresser drawer. Sadness crept in as he recalled every word he'd memorized.

Dear Son,
If you're reading this, then I have left this earth. I
know I haven't always been the best father or made
the best decisions, but I want you to know that I
love you. I am proud of you. Proud of the man you
are becoming. A man so much better than me.
Emerson

With shaky hands, Wyatt slipped the single sheet of
paper from the envelope and read the letter Emerson
Monroe had written to his friend George.

George,
Watch over my son. See that he makes good decisions and exercises good judgment. Traits you have
that I don't. Thank you for being a good friend.
Emerson

Wyatt wasn't sure how he felt about the note or the
fact that his father had asked his friend to "watch over"
him. Had George stayed on the ranch all these years
out of duty to Wyatt's father? He felt as if he'd taken a
hoof in the gut. Memories of all the times Wyatt told
George to worry about his own responsibilities while
Wyatt took care of the day-to-day running of the ranch
horrified him.

He opened the book to replace the letter and envelope. A small scrap of paper fell out. He picked it up and
stared at the numbers written across the front.

41557922-104952393

He turned the scrap of paper over. Blank on the
other side.

"Do you know about this upcoming town-hall meeting?"

Jackie's question drew his attention away from the strange numbers. "There's one a month. Nothing special about them. Mostly a chance for folks to get together. Why?"

She held up a flyer just like the one he had at home. She flipped it over. "Look at this."

In big, bold letters were the words *KEEP YOUR MOUTH SHUT OR ELSE.*

Tucking the piece of paper back into the book, he crossed to her side. "Sounds like a warning."

"Yep. And whatever George knew got him killed."

"Why didn't Landers find it?"

"It was stuck to the back of a *National Geographic* magazine." She pulled out her cell phone. "Time to call the sheriff."

Twenty minutes later they greeted Landers in the driveway.

"What are you two doing out here?" Landers asked.

Wyatt's defenses bristled at the accusing tone in his stepfather's voice. "I own the house."

Landers cut him a sharp glance. "I'm well aware of that. However, you shouldn't be anywhere near the place, not while you're still a person of interest in the investigation." He pinned Jackie with a hard look. "You should know this."

She shrugged, clearly unrepentant. "I'm a private citizen now. Came here with the property owner. No laws were broken."

Jackie had said something before about having been in law enforcement. At the time he hadn't thought too much about it, but now he was curious to know in what capacity she had served.

"It doesn't look good," Landers groused.

"Murder's never pretty, boss," Jackie shot back.

Wyatt fought the urge to laugh. He really liked her spunk.

"We did find something of interest, though," she said.

Landers's gray eyes widened. "You went inside and searched the house?"

"To make sure whoever trashed the place wasn't still lurking about," Jackie stated. She held up the flyer for the town meeting with her gloved hand. "I'd say George had an enemy. We just need to find out who."

"Not *we,* Ms. Blain," Landers said in an adamant tone. "You two stay away from my investigation."

"Some would consider you investigating your stepson a conflict of interest," Jackie said, her tone bland.

Landers narrowed his gaze. "I've already put in a call to the state police. They'll be sending someone over to assist."

Jackie's mouth quirked. "Good to know."

Landers reached into his pocket for a handkerchief and used it to take the flyer from Jackie's hands. "Now, I suggest you two go back to the main house and stay there. Let me do my job."

With a snap, Jackie yanked off the plastic gloves. "Have you found the primary crime scene yet?"

Exasperation crossed Landers's face. "Stop fishing, Ms. Blain. You know I can't divulge information on an ongoing investigation."

Jackie's lips twisted in a wry half smile. "I'll take that as a no."

"Why do you say that?" Wyatt asked, finding their banter entertaining and informative.

"Because if they had found the place where George had been murdered, then they would be asking you questions to see if they could place you at the scene. But because you're still walking around a free man, I'm guessing they have yet to determine George's whereabouts the night of his death."

Landers looked at Wyatt, his gray eyes probing, almost pleading. "Wyatt, for your mother's sake, please don't do anything to throw any more suspicion on yourself. Stay close to home and out of my way."

With that, Landers strode away, carrying the threatening note by the corner. Wyatt stared after him, pleased by Landers's show of concern for his mother's peace of mind.

"What's up with you and your mom?" Jackie asked, peering at him intently.

"I haven't talked to her." The last thing he needed was to deal with his mother. Her calls had increased in the past twenty-four hours. She'd want to smother him with concern and demand an explanation. Just as she had the night Dina had died. But he wasn't willing to tell anyone what happened that horrible night. No matter what.

Jackie tucked her arm around Wyatt's and led him to his 4x4. "Come on, cowboy, we've another stop to make before we do as the sheriff asks."

Half an hour later, they stood at the fence line on the southwest corner of the property. The fresh snow from last night's storm had covered the tire tracks of the motorcycle. They drove along the fence for several yards but saw no signs of damage or tampering.

"Our mysterious cyclist most likely doubled back and left the property," Jackie said. She had her hands jammed into the pockets of her parka. Wild blond curls stuck out from beneath the edges of her bright pink beanie. Her cheeks were rosy and her eyes were bright in the winter sun.

Attraction flared and he tamped it down because the last thing he needed was to be distracted by her beauty.

"What form of law enforcement were you in?" he asked.

She met his gaze. "I was a deputy sheriff in Atkins, Iowa."

That explained the driving. But then again, being from Boston also explained her driving. He shook his head. "You're just full of surprises."

Her grin knocked him back a step. Keeping himself immune to her charms was proving impossible.

"I like to keep things interesting."

Though his mouth felt as if he had cotton balls stuffed into his cheeks, he asked, "What made you decide to go into law enforcement?"

With a shrug, she said, "I wanted excitement. I grew up watching reruns of *Charlie's Angels.* The original series." Her grin widened. "I wanted to carry a gun."

Warning bells clanged in his head. This wasn't a girl who wanted to shoot pop cans off fence posts with a pelt gun. She wanted to chase drug runners and wear spandex. What was spandex, anyhow? All he knew was that it melted next to Wyoming campfires. He adjusted his hat. "And which character did you want to be?"

He was sure she'd say Farah Fawcett's. She was an icon even beyond the TV show.

"Sabrina."

The tomboy. Okay, so much for thinking he could predict anything about Jackie Blain. "Why?"

"She was the smartest, the most savvy and the one who saved the day more than the others."

He couldn't say whether her assessment was true or not. He'd only seen the show a few times. And only to watch Farrah. "Why did you change professions?"

Her expression grew pensive. "Personal reasons."

Concern hit him like a cold wind across the plain. "Were you injured?"

The thought of a bullet tearing through her perfect skin slammed through him, making his fist curl to keep himself from reaching out to her.

She let out a humorless laugh. "No. Nothing like that."

Hardness settled in her blue eyes, making them shine like crystal. She looked away, and he glimpsed a shadow of hurt. Something bad had happened to her, something that still caused her pain. But apparently she had no intention of sharing her inner turmoil with him.

Which was fine with him. He had enough of his own secret torments. He didn't want to take on anyone else's.

Yet he couldn't stop the welling compassion making him want to take her in his arms and soothe away whatever haunted her.

He jammed his hands into his pockets.

An uncomfortable silence stretched between them.

"We should get back to the house for lunch," he finally said when he couldn't take the tension any longer. "Gabby'll be wondering about us."

"I'm sure she's having fun with Spencer," Jackie said, her expression clearing, her smile tender. "He's getting spoiled with so much attention. I'm afraid when we go back home he'll be one sad puppy."

Wyatt had a feeling there would be several sad people, too.

When they arrived back at the ranch, Wyatt put the book he'd taken from George's house on the bookshelf in the living room. He supposed he should have okayed it with the sheriff, but because the book belonged to the Monroe family, Wyatt didn't see the need to ask permission. He'd apologize later if need be.

Gabby skidded to a stop in the doorway. "Daddy!" she squealed and ran toward him.

He scooped her up into his arms. White powder dusted her nose, and a smear of chocolate ran the length of her chin. "What have you been up to?"

"I made chocolate-chip cookies," she said with pride.

He lifted his nose to smell the air. "Hmm. I can smell them baking. What a big girl you are to be making cookies."

She grinned. "I am a big girl."

There was a knock at the front door. Wyatt set Gabby down. "Go on back to the kitchen," he directed her and headed toward the living room as Penny came out of the kitchen, wiping her hands on an apron.

"I'll get it," Wyatt said. He reached for the doorknob and opened the door.

The man standing on the porch wore a thick wool coat

over a navy blue suit, white dress shirt, red power tie and black, shiny wing tips. His salted hair was barely visible beneath the wool watch cap pulled low over his ears.

"Good afternoon, Wyatt," Richard Pendleton said.

Irritation sluiced through Wyatt's blood. This was the fourth time in the past month the man had shown up uninvited on his porch.

The first time, Wyatt heard him out. The man represented a mining corporation. The Degas Group wanted to buy the mineral rights to his property and the transportation rights to use it during the mining of his neighbors' land.

Wyatt had no intention of agreeing to either request. "What are you doing here? My answer has not changed."

"May I come in?" he asked, undaunted. His expression was polite, his gaze friendly.

"I'd rather you didn't. We have nothing to talk about."

"You may want this to go away, but it's not going to. Your neighbors won't let it. We'll double our offer," he said.

They'd already offered him a half a million dollars. Now they wanted to give him a million? For rights that may or may not pan out.

Neither he nor his father before him had ever allowed any type of surveying on the Monroe ranch. Wyatt had too much respect for the land to even contemplate robbing the soil of the minerals God had enriched it with, whatever they may be. Nor was he going to allow outsiders to use the road his father had built and grant his neighbors access to it out of a sense of community.

"No."

The congenial facade dropped. Pendleton narrowed

his brown eyes. His voice dipped to a menacing growl. "You won't be able to keep the land tied up forever, Mr. Monroe."

FIVE

Wyatt took a step forward. Adrenaline surged through his blood. "Is that a threat?"

Pendleton held up his hands. "Just saying. We know you're barely making payroll as it is."

Wyatt's fingers curled. "My finances are nobody's business but mine."

"Wouldn't you rather secure your daughter's future by putting a nice chunk of change away for her?"

"My daughter's future will be just fine." His father had taught him to be a shrewd businessman and rancher.

Besides the cattle, horses and hay that brought in income to the ranch, he traded stocks and had built up a nice personal portfolio that he kept separate from the Monroe holdings. He had more than enough to cover Gabby's education at any of the top colleges in the country, including a graduate degree if she chose to go that route. He didn't need to compromise his principles for money.

"I hear you had a bit of trouble lately," Richard said. "The murder of your ranch hand must be bad for business."

Wyatt dipped his chin and stared at the man. "Did you have something to do with George's death?"

"Me?" Richard scoffed. "Rumor has it you're the one the police are looking at. What happens if you go to jail? Who's going to protect your ranch and your daughter when you use all your resources for legal fees?"

Wyatt's temper flared. He held on to it by a thin string. "Get off my property and do not return."

"Or what? I'll end up like your poor ranch hand?"

Wyatt took a step forward. "Leave."

"Fine. I'll see you at the town-hall meeting." With that, Pendleton rapidly retreated, nearly knocking Jackie over in the process. Wyatt hadn't seen her approach; he'd been too focused on the slimy city slicker.

"What did that guy want?" she asked as she followed Wyatt inside.

"Nothing important."

"Hmm, not buying that." She shimmied past him and blocked his way. She made a formidable barrier. "Tell me what's going on. That man made some statements that could be deemed threatening. And given recent events…"

Wyatt ran a hand through his hair. "He represents a mining company that has been after me to sell them the mineral rights on the Monroe ranch. And transportation rights for the neighbors' land."

"What kinds of minerals are in the ground here?"

"Don't know. Not something I'm interested in finding out. Because even if there was a vein of gold, I wouldn't allow any mining."

"Admirable stance. How do you suppose he heard about your trouble?"

He arched an eyebrow. "This is a small town. People talk."

Her lips twisted, drawing his gaze. She had nice lips, soft looking, plump. Kissable.

He blinked, taken aback by where his mind was going.

The more time he spent with her, the harder it was to resist the attraction between them.

Okay, so he couldn't help being attracted. A normal reaction given she was a beautiful woman and, well, he was a red-blooded male.

She had curves in the right places and a pretty face that he could get used to looking at day in and day out. And that head of hair. He wanted to bury his hands in that mass of curls and see if the strands were as silky as they appeared. He wanted to wrap the stray curl teasing her mouth around his finger and tug her closer.

Whoa, not happening.

He jerked his gaze and his thoughts away from that treacherous path.

"I think we should head to that town-hall meeting," Jackie said.

Bringing his gaze back to her, he nodded. "All right. But I have to warn you, these things are pretty dull."

"I can handle it. Besides, if Mr. Mining Guy is going to be there, you'll want to make sure you are, too."

The town-hall meeting was held in the basement of the library. Jackie followed Wyatt inside the window-less room. Metal folding chairs had been set up in rows, and a podium with a microphone stood at the head of the room. Most of the seats were already taken. People called out greetings to one another. The din of chatter echoed off the walls. The scene reminded her of town meetings back in Atkins. She guessed most small towns were the same in many respects.

As people noticed Wyatt enter, the chatter died down to a low roar. Jackie frowned at the stares and whispered comments. Her protective instincts charged to life. She wanted to stand on a chair and chastise the townsfolk for behaving so badly.

If Wyatt noticed the change in the atmosphere of the room, he didn't show it. He folded his long frame onto a seat at the end of a middle row. Jackie slid past him to take the seat next to him.

A few minutes later, a heavyset man took the podium.

"Welcome, everyone, to our March town-hall meeting. For those of you who don't know me, I'm Mayor Jay Whitehead. We have several items on the agenda today. But first, we have a guest here tonight—the representative from Degas Group. He'd like to have a moment of your time before we get started with town business."

The man who'd visited the ranch house stepped up to the mic. "I'm Richard Pendleton. I've spoken with many of you over the past few months. As some of you know, the Degas Group is a mining corporation based out of Cheyenne. We believe the land here in Lane County is rich in minerals. We'd like the opportunity to partner with you to mine the soil and make us all a little richer."

Wyatt snorted under his breath.

A thought occurred to Jackie. If the corporation was pushing this hard, they had to have some idea what was beneath the ground. And whatever it was must be worth a pretty penny because she doubted the Degas Group would be interested in making money for other people out of the kindness of their hearts.

"I'm ready to sell, but a certain someone won't," an elderly man grumbled loudly from somewhere behind Jackie.

Richard nodded. "It's true that we have some members of your community who are opposed to the idea of mining the earth, but we assure you we are committed to preserving the land and doing as little damage as possible in our mining operations."

"It's Wyatt Monroe who's ruining everything. He's keeping the rest of us from profiting from our own land!" a woman shouted.

"That's true," another voice called out. "I'm ready to sell now, but unless I can use the access road across his property, they won't buy."

"I thought he murdered George!" A lanky man jumped to his feet and pointed at Wyatt. "Why isn't he locked up?"

The room erupted as others joined in, wanting to know why Wyatt hadn't been arrested and put in jail. Why wouldn't Wyatt sell his rights? Why wouldn't he allow his neighbors to use his roads?

Jackie's temper boiled. She started to rise, but Wyatt's hand restrained her. She turned to stare at him. He shook his head, his brooding gaze hurt but resigned. With a huff, she settled back down but her fingers curled.

"Please, please," Jay said, holding up a hand. "Calm yourselves. Sheriff Landers would like to address the issue raised by Boyd Dunn."

Jackie was glad to have a name to put to the rabble-rouser.

Sheriff Landers stepped up to the microphone. "There has been no arrest made in the murder of George Herman. This is an ongoing investigation. The state police have sent officers to assist in the investigation." He pinned several people with direct looks. "I would like to remind you all that guilt is proven in a court of law, not in rumors and speculation."

Surprised to hear the sheriff sticking up for Wyatt, she turned to see his reaction. Or rather, lack of reaction. He stared impassively at the sheriff. But then she realized his jaw had firmed to a hard line. Not as unaffected as he'd like everyone to think.

Boyd Dunn practically foamed at the mouth. "But he murdered his wife! He murdered Dina! Surely you have to take that into account!"

Stunned by the accusation, Jackie jerked her gaze to Wyatt's. She saw guilt and sadness in the swirling dark depths of his eyes, making her blood run cold.

He murdered his wife.

The echo of the accusation ricocheted off the concrete walls of the library's basement and slammed into her, forcing the breath from her lungs.

Could it be true? Had Wyatt murdered his wife?

After a heartbeat of silence, the room erupted again.

Uncle Carl quickly stood and came to Wyatt's defense. The mayor asked for silence and was ignored. Others debated Wyatt's guilt and innocence. Everything faded to white noise as Jackie stared into Wyatt's dark eyes.

She willed him to jump to his feet and deny the allegation.

But he didn't. No defense tumbled from his lips. His

seemingly dispassionate gaze never altered. His posture didn't change. Only the subtle tightening of his jaw betrayed a reaction.

It was enough to make Jackie want to defend him. The man she was coming to know was a devoted father, was a fair boss to his employees and had a conscience.

But the words stuck in her throat. She'd seen a whole lot of guilty during her time as a sheriff's deputy. Enough to make believing in a man's innocence first a tough row to hoe.

Maybe this time she saw what she wanted to see.

She'd witnessed firsthand how evil hid behind all sorts of facades. The philanthropist who embezzled money from his employees. The soccer mom who dealt drugs. The churchgoing father who beat his wife and kids.

As a bodyguard, she'd protected clients from stalkers who looked like the boy next door, from corporate CEOs who wanted to crush a whistle-blower, from a vengeful ex-con out to kill the person who'd been instrumental in sending him to prison.

Evil prowled like a hungry tiger, eating away at the hearts and souls of those who let it in. Had Wyatt let evil in? What did she really know about him?

She knew he was a widower. Knew his wife died three years ago, but Jackie didn't know how she'd died. The cause of death hadn't been important to the current situation.

Now she had to know. But not here, not like this.

Until she learned the details, she'd give him the benefit of the doubt. Innocent until proven guilty. That was the way justice was supposed to work—in a perfect world, at least.

Her gaze slid to the man who'd so passionately accused Wyatt of murder. Rangy with sandy-blond hair beneath a baseball cap, the man's features were sharp with angles and planes. He glared at Wyatt with palpable malice and resumed his seat. Was he a relative of Wyatt's deceased wife?

Jackie turned her attention to the man from the mining company, who was leaning against the wall. After witnessing the animosity between Wyatt and the Degas Corporation's representative, the smug look on Pendleton's face wasn't surprising. The anger his smugness evoked within her chest caught her off guard.

Her fingers curled into even tighter fists. She hated to see anyone enjoying another person's pain. Had he prompted Boyd's accusation?

A loud whistle brought all the chaotic noise to an abrupt halt. The sheriff removed two fingers from his lips to say, "Please, everyone, settle down. We will not discuss the past. If you have issues with the law, you can come to my office."

The mayor took over the microphone. "Okay, people, we have a full agenda. Moving on now, let's talk about the Easter Parade."

A hand on her arm set her senses on alert. Wyatt leaned close. "You'll need to ride back with your uncle."

The musky, pleasant scent of his aftershave distracted her, so it took a moment for his words to sink in. By then he'd risen and strode toward the exit, his head held high and his back ramrod straight. If he was aware of the glares following him, he didn't acknowledge them. Jackie scrambled from her seat and hurried after him.

Just as Wyatt reached the exit, a woman stepped up and touched his arm. Surprise washed over Jackie as she noted the resemblance between Wyatt and the older woman. She had to be his mother. She wore a brown shearling coat over jeans and a purple turtleneck sweater. Her brunet hair was cut in a short bob, and her dark eyes brimmed with sympathy.

Wyatt stalled for a fraction of a second. His back was to Jackie, so she couldn't see his expression, but there was no mistaking the stiffening of his shoulders. He patted his mom's hand, then continued out the door.

Hurt twisted his mother's face. Empathy knotted in Jackie's chest. As she passed the older woman, their gazes collided. Jackie gave her a polite smile as she headed toward the door to follow Wyatt, but his mom stepped into Jackie's path.

"Hello. I'm Wyatt's mother, Marsha. My husband told me who you are and why you're here," Marsha said. "I appreciate that you're helping Wyatt. He needs someone on his side who he'll listen to."

Not sure what to say in response, Jackie nodded.

"He can be so stubborn," she continued.

"I've noticed." Antsy to find Wyatt, Jackie took a side step.

"I don't believe he killed George." Marsha lowered her voice.

Jackie didn't think so, either. But his wife…?

"I should go." She hustled out the door. Outside, the late-afternoon sunlight glistened off the snow-covered roofs and made Jackie squint and raise a hand to shield her eyes. She quickly located Wyatt climbing into his truck.

"Wyatt!" she called out.

He slammed the door without acknowledging her. Annoyance shot through her bloodstream. If the man thought he could ignore or outrun her, he was sorely mistaken.

One way or another, he was going to talk to her. And then she'd decide how to proceed.

Wyatt glanced in the rearview mirror as he drove away from the library. Jackie stood on the sidewalk, hands on hips, feet braced apart. Her wild curls lifted slightly on the afternoon breeze. His jaw clenched, and he let out a groan. She'd followed him out of the town-hall meeting. He wasn't really surprised; she didn't seem the sort to let a bomb like the one Boyd lobbed at him go without an explanation.

And just like with everyone else who'd asked what happened that night, he would explain what he could and keep the rest tightly locked up in a box within his soul because the pain, the humiliation would be too much to bear. He'd rather feel nothing than relive the past.

He lifted his foot off the gas for a fraction of a second. It wasn't his habit to leave behind the one he'd brought to the party. But the thought of being trapped inside the cab of the truck with Jackie's inquisitive questions and all-too-perceptive blue eyes added pressure to the heavy weight sitting on his chest. He was barely controlling the fierce rage threatening to explode as it was. The last thing he needed was to have his self-appointed defender probing his old wound. Especially after the wary suspicion he'd seen in her gaze as she'd stared at him. Her pretty face had hardened, revealing the cop inside. Her probing would hurt.

Lifting his gaze to the Snowy Range Mountains, which provided a stunning backdrop to Lane County, he looked for inspiration. None came.

A wave of hurt washed over him. How had he become the bad guy?

He wished he could pray. That he could find some solace in faith. It wasn't that he didn't believe or that he and God were estranged. He just didn't know what to say anymore. No words would form, even as a deep welling of pain choked him.

The past couldn't be undone. He couldn't change the hearts of the townspeople. He couldn't even allow himself to hope the future would ever be better.

The peace he'd built around himself and Gabby had been demolished when he'd found George murdered on his front porch. The shock still reverberated through him like the ripples of a stone dropping into a pool of water.

And once again, the townsfolk were quick to point a finger at him, eager to believe him capable of murder, willing to accept his guilt when the evidence wasn't there to support any culpability.

He couldn't deny he'd been a wild, angry young man growing up. He had engaged in numerous fights as a teen and had had many scrapes with the law. Or rather, his stepfather. Wasn't his fault they were one and the same.

But he wasn't that same rebel. He was a rancher, employing ten people. He was also a father. The most important thing he could ever be.

When would he stop paying for his immature mistakes? When would he stop feeling guilty for Dina's death?

When would he ever be free to feel anything but cold numbness in his heart? Never.

Not even for a feisty blonde.

Jackie would have to get a ride back to the ranch with her uncle. He stepped on the gas and drove away.

Jackie jumped out of her uncle's older-model 4x4 and stalked toward the main house. The whole drive back from town, her uncle refused to say anything about Wyatt's ex-wife other than that it wasn't his tale to tell. Even searching the internet on her phone hadn't yielded enough information to answer her questions. The news account stated Dina Monroe died in an accidental fall.

Had Wyatt killed his wife? How had she fallen? Was it an accident or murder? What was the official cause of death? What had their relationship been like?

And what did any of this have to do with the current situation?

SIX

Jackie tried to curb the curiosity that the afternoon had stirred as she knocked on the front door of Wyatt's home. She heard his muffled, "Come in!"

Stepping inside, she saw he wasn't in the living room. Nor the kitchen. The door to his home office was closed. Squaring her shoulders, she opened the door and peeked inside. Wyatt wasn't in there, either.

She took a moment to absorb the emptiness of the room. The overhead light was off, but ambient light came in through the open curtain. The room was definitely masculine in tone. The walls were painted soft beige, and a leather captain's chair sat behind a desk and computer station. A bookcase was propped against one wall, though it didn't hold books but rows of thick binders.

She moved away from the office to the bottom of the stairs. "Wyatt?"

"Upstairs!"

She ascended the stairs and walked to the open doorway about halfway down the hall.

Gabby's room. Pink walls, ruffled light pink curtains and frilly bed coverings with a mound of stuffed animals making a home along the foot of the four-poster bed. It was any little girl's dream room. In the center of the floor stood a small round table with a plastic purple tea service and four equally small chairs, two of which were occupied.

Wyatt sat across from Gabby, his knees bent high as he leaned in to let Gabby pour imaginary tea into the tiny cup in his much larger hand.

Jackie's heart stuttered and sighed. The pair looked so sweet together. The sight of this big, macho man sitting at this child-size table, daintily having a tea party with his four-year-old daughter, whose face beamed with joy, brought a rush of emotion to the surface within Jackie's soul. Affection, tenderness and yearning mixed to form a lump in her throat.

Gabby's red curls stuck out beneath the tiara perched atop her head. She stared at her father with adoration on her pixie face.

Wyatt glanced Jackie's way with a sheepish smile. "We're taking high tea."

Her heart did a little flutter. "I see that."

Gabby held up the teapot. "You want some?"

"Please join us," Wyatt added, pulling back a chair for her.

"I'd like that." Jackie sat on the edge of the seat. Her knees bumped the table. "Oops, sorry."

"No worries," Wyatt said. "Tea?" He handed her a cup and saucer.

"Yes, thank you." She held out the cup for Gabby to pour. "I like your crown."

"You want one?" Gabby asked.

"Sure, I'd love one." Jackie shared a tender glance

with Wyatt as Gabby jumped up and ran to a small trunk. She flipped open the lid and dug around. When she came back, she had a more elaborate crown in one hand and a white feather boa in the other. She reached up to plop the circlet onto Jackie's head and then wrapped the boa around her shoulders.

"I feel like such a pretty princess," Jackie said.

Gabby shook her head. "You're not a princess. I'm the princess."

"Oh. Then what am I?"

"You're the queen!" Gabby exclaimed and sat down.

Catching the twinkle in Wyatt's eyes, Jackie said, "Am I, now? How wonderful. Is your father my minion, then?"

Gabby tilted her head. "Minion?"

Wyatt grinned as he explained, "She means her gofer."

Wrinkling her nose, Gabby shook her head. "He's not an animal. He's the prince."

"Ah, I see," Jackie said, nearly bursting with the effort to maintain a straight face as laughter welled inside her. "Does the prince have to do the queen's bidding?"

Gabby blinked, then looked to her father for an explanation.

"She wants to know if the prince has to obey the queen."

A wide smile spread across Gabby's face. She clapped her hands. "Oh, yes. The prince obeys the queen. Everyone obeys the queen."

Jackie liked the sound of that. Pretending to take a sip of tea to keep from hooting outright, Jackie held Wyatt's gaze. "Indeed."

He lifted one dark eyebrow. "As you wish, my lady."

Liking this playful side of him, she grinned. "We could use some cookies, don't you think?"

Wyatt nodded. "Cookies would add so much to our tea. A certain princess I know made some very delicious chocolate-chip cookies."

Gabby bounced in her chair. "Yeah! Cookies."

He unfolded himself from the chair. "I'll be right back."

As he passed Jackie, she was sure his hand brushed her shoulder. She turned to watch him stride from the room. Tall and proud. A man who loved his daughter.

A dark cloud passed over the sunshine he'd brought into her life so unexpectedly. But was he a murderer?

Giving her head a shake, she looked at Gabby and smiled. "You don't have a boa. Don't princesses wear feathers?"

"I have only one boa." Her face lit up. "But I do have a cape. Can a princess wear a cape?"

"Of course."

Gabby retrieved a red velvet cape. Jackie leaned over to help her tie the string. "There, now. Princess Gabby."

The sound of the doorbell chimed. A moment later Jackie heard the rumble of Wyatt's deep voice. Then other men. Something was going on downstairs.

"The queen needs to go see what's keeping the prince." She rose. "You stay right here, okay, sweetie?"

Gabby frowned. "Can't I come, too?"

"No, it'd be best if the princess…" The sound of the front door closing cut off the voices. They'd gone outside. She needed to get down there. Her gaze landed on a stuffed bear. She crossed the room and plucked the toy from the end of Gabby's bed, brought it back to the table and secured him in Wyatt's vacant chair. "Mr. Bear would like some tea."

"And Mrs. Rabbit?"

Holding on to her patience, Jackie grabbed a big white rabbit wearing a dress from the bed and positioned the animal at the table. "There, now. I'll go see about the cookies."

Leaving Gabby to pour pretend tea for the stuffed animals, Jackie hurried downstairs and out the front door in time to see the sheriff putting Wyatt into the backseat of his cruiser. Another man sat in the passenger seat. He was dressed in a different uniform than the sheriff. She guessed he must be the state investigator. She rushed down the porch stairs.

"Hold on a minute!" she shouted.

The sheriff paused as he rounded the back of the cruiser. His eyebrows rose as he took in her attire. "Playing dress up?"

Ignoring his question and the feathers tickling her chin, she gestured to Wyatt. "What are you doing? Why are you taking him in?"

The sheriff sighed. "I know you want to help, Ms. Blain. The best thing you can do for Wyatt is to stay with Gabby."

"You didn't answer my question."

"You aren't his attorney," he stated. "Though it would probably be a good idea if you called Mr. Kelly and had him meet us at the station."

Not about to let the sheriff keep her in the dark, she blocked his steps to the driver's side door. "What are you charging him with?"

"We're not charging him with anything yet. We're only bringing him back in for questioning."

Her mind worked possible scenarios. It was too soon for the DNA to come back on the knife. A witness? Or... "You found the primary crime scene."

His jaw tightened. "Call his lawyer, Ms. Blain." With that, he slid into the driver's seat and drove away.

She met Wyatt's gaze through the back passenger window. The bleakness in his eyes cut a cold path through her. She couldn't let him be railroaded into a murder charge. She had to do something.

First, though, she needed to make sure Gabby was safe and cared for. Securing Aunt Penny took precious minutes as her aunt peppered her with questions she didn't have the answers to. Then she took off toward town in her rented SUV. On the way she called her boss.

"Jackie, I trust you're spending your vacation relaxing?" James Trent asked.

"Not exactly." She quickly explained the situation. "I'm headed to the sheriff's station now."

There was a moment of silence before James cleared his throat. "I can appreciate that you feel the need to help this man because of your love for your aunt and uncle, but might I remind you, you are no longer in law enforcement? You need to back off and let the authorities do their jobs. Your role is to be the dutiful niece. Not the cop or the bodyguard."

She winced as his words sank in. Logically, she knew he was right.

What was her role here? Her aunt and uncle wanted her to investigate, to prove Wyatt innocent. But she had no authority to do that. Sheriff Landers had already chastised her once for interfering.

Wyatt wasn't a protectee. There hadn't been any real threat to his life, if you discounted a possible murder charge and someone following them.

The image of Wyatt and Gabby sitting at the little table having a tea party knotted her stomach.

The best way to help Wyatt and Gabby was to call his lawyer and pray that God would see them through this.

Wyatt sat across from the state investigator, answering the same questions he'd answered two days ago for Sheriff Landers. The answers had not changed.

Hopefully they'd realize he was telling the truth soon and let him go home to Gabby. His heart contracted in his chest. He hadn't been given a chance to tell her goodbye before being shoved into the back of the sheriff's car and driven to town.

But Jackie knew.

And he trusted she'd take care of Gabby. That gave him some measure of peace. His daughter was safe with the pretty blonde.

"So the last time you saw George was the day before his murder?"

Barely able to keep a hold on his temper, Wyatt gritted out, "Yes. I've already said this. Twice now. He was fine. He was heading into town to buy Gabby's Easter present."

That was one thing Wyatt could always count on George for—spoiling Gabby every chance he got. Like the Kirks, George had taken it upon himself to be a surrogate grandfather to Gabby.

George's killer was still at large, and the longer the police wasted time trying to pin his murder on Wyatt, the less likely it would be they'd find the real culprit and make an arrest.

"And you didn't go to town that night?"

"No. Like I said, I was home with Gabby."

"Is there anyone who can confirm that?"

Obviously a four-year-old wasn't a reliable alibi. "I'm sure if I'd left, the Kirks would have noticed."

The state investigator, a thin, balding man with sharp features and sharper hazel eyes, made a note on the pad of paper in front of him. He'd introduced himself as Special Agent Ed Harrison. "You stayed in the whole night?"

"Yes. The whole night."

"Have you ever been to the Whiskey Saloon?"

Wyatt blinked. That was a new question. "Not in a long time."

Harrison narrowed his gaze. "How long?"

"More than ten years."

"Why?"

Wyatt frowned. "Why what?"

"Why haven't you been to the Whiskey Saloon in ten years?"

Clamping his teeth together, Wyatt fought back the burn of anger. "The last time I set foot in the Whiskey Saloon was to drag my drunk father home."

The episode was etched in Wyatt's memory like the carvings on a tree trunk. Faded but never totally gone. Wyatt had received a call from Bill Smith, the proprietor of the Whiskey Saloon, telling him he'd better come take his father away before he drank himself to death.

Removing him from the bar hadn't prevented him from drowning his sorrows in drink. He'd died of liver failure not long after that day.

"You didn't go to the Whiskey Saloon the night of March 18?"

"No. I didn't. Why?"

"Someone matching your description was seen talking to Mr. Herman in the parking lot."

Wyatt blinked. "Wasn't me."

A knock on the interrogation room door startled Wyatt. The door swung open, and Bruce Kelly walked in. "I demand you cease questioning my client."

Harrison leaned back in the metal folding chair. "Your client didn't ask for a phone call or for his lawyer."

But Sheriff Landers had suggested to Jackie that she call him. Wyatt had heard it from the back of the cruiser, so surely the state investigator had, too. But technically, Harrison was correct. Wyatt hadn't asked for Mr. Kelly because he'd had every confidence Jackie would.

Kelly's lips pressed together as he shot Wyatt an annoyed look. Clearly Kelly thought Wyatt should have asked for him. "I'm here now. I'd like a moment alone with my client."

"Of course." Harrison stood and strode from the room.

Kelly set his briefcase on the table and took the seat recently vacated by the state investigator. "Why didn't you call me?"

"How did you know to come?" Though Wyatt had a pretty good idea how the lawyer heard he was needed. Jackie.

"Look, they have a witness claiming to have seen

you with George just prior to the time the medical examiner says he was killed. You need to level with me. Were you with George?"

Tired of being falsely accused of murder, he bit out, "No. I wasn't."

Kelly nodded. "Unfortunately, we can't corroborate your alibi. Penny and Carl Kirk didn't hear you leave, but they can't swear that you were at the house, though they are certain you wouldn't have left your daughter alone. However, that would not hold up in court."

"In other words, I'm sunk since they have an eyewitness, and everyone would rather believe this person than me."

"Not necessarily."

"Do I get to know who's accusing me?"

Kelly consulted his notes. "Mrs. Southworth. Her apartment faces the back alley of the Whiskey Saloon. She saw George come out the back door. A tall man wearing a cowboy hat approached George and led him away."

"That describes half the men in this town."

Kelly made a noncommittal gesture. "But how many other men would George willingly leave with?"

"You don't believe me, either?"

"I didn't say that." Kelly took off his glasses and rubbed the bridge of his nose for a second before replacing them. "Would you consider taking a polygraph test?"

Anger churned in his gut. A lie-detector test. "Sure, if that's what it takes to prove my innocence."

"I'll make the arrangements." Kelly stood. "Don't worry, Wyatt. You'll get through this."

"Yeah, thanks."

Left alone in the interrogation room, Wyatt massaged his temples. He'd get through this. It seemed as though that was all he was ever doing—getting through life as best he could.

But would his best be good enough? He could only pray that it would be.

Jackie arrived at the sheriff's station just as the sun was setting. She had a strange sense of déjà vu as she entered the redbrick building. Had it really been only two days since she'd first stepped into Wyatt Monroe's life?

She spotted the lawyer, Bruce Kelly, and blocked his path. "Did they find the primary crime scene? Is that why they hauled Wyatt back here?"

He grimly shook his head and explained.

"That's what they're holding him on?" Flimsy at best. "Why aren't you demanding they release him?"

"I will," he shot back. "Wyatt has agreed to a polygraph. I'm on my way now to arrange it."

"Even if he passes, you know it won't hold up in court if this should go to trial," she stated. She'd seen people pass the lie-detector test and be as guilty as could be.

"In Wyoming they are admissible, to a degree. If he takes the test and passes—"

"He'll pass."

He held up a hand. "I have no doubt he will. However, we need this to convince the state investigator."

"Fine. Did the state guy agree to it?"

"Yes."

"Then get the test done quickly. His daughter needs him."

Kelly nodded and marched away.

Jackie strode toward the desk where a sergeant manned the reception area. "I'd like to speak with the sheriff."

The sergeant eyed her for a moment, then picked up the phone. "Hey, that lady's here."

So he'd been expecting her. Go figure. A couple minutes passed before the sheriff ambled out of an office and made his way to her. "What can I do for you, Ms. Blain?"

As if he didn't know. "I'd like to talk to Wyatt."

"Sorry. No visitors."

"Why are you doing this? He's your stepson. Don't you have any love for him? For Gabby?"

He gripped her by the elbow and tugged her away from the curious stares of the officers nearby. He lowered his voice. "Of course I do. But I can't be breaking rules for him. The state's investigator is here. He's calling the shots."

"Then let me talk to him," she insisted.

"And say what? What can you possibly do for Wyatt?"

Her boss's words rang in her head. *Your role is to be the dutiful niece. Not the cop or the bodyguard.*

What about friend? Wyatt was in sore need of a friend right now. Someone who believed him.

What if he murdered his wife? The doubts and suspicions reared.

"Tell me about Wyatt's wife."

Sheriff Landers scowled. "Her death was ruled an accident."

"Then why do people think he killed her?"

He rubbed a hand over his jaw. "You know how people are. The husband is always suspected in the death of a spouse."

What he said was true, but he was holding something back. "Did you know Wyatt agreed to a polygraph?"

His eyebrows twitched. "I didn't. But that's good. That will at least clear him and steer the investigation in a different direction."

"Which direction? Do you have other suspects? Have you looked into the Degas Corporation? They have a motive to hurt Wyatt. What about Pendleton, the representative? Did you ask him where he was the night George was murdered?"

One thing Jackie knew for sure: murder could be as complicated as it was simple. She had a feeling everything about this case was complicated. It would be simpler if Wyatt were the culprit and much more complicated if a big, multimillion-dollar corporation had anything to do with George's murder.

SEVEN

Sheriff Landers's expression closed, shutting Jackie out. "I can't discuss this with you, Ms. Blain. I suggest you return to the ranch and wait for Wyatt to be released."

She shook her head in frustration. "I'm not going anywhere until you release Wyatt."

His facial features softened, and he sighed. "You might have a long wait."

"That's fine. I can be patient when I need to be." Which wasn't often.

He tipped his chin in acknowledgment and walked away. Jackie found a bench to park herself on. She knew it could be hours before Wyatt was released. A polygraph test took two or three, and that was only if the Lane County sheriff's department had a tester and the equipment in-house. If they had to wait for someone to come from another county or state even, then it could be tomorrow or longer before he was released. She closed her eyes and silently prayed.

As it turned out, she only had to wait five hours, which consisted of five cups of coffee, a bag of chips, a Danish and power reading every magazine and newspaper she could find in the police station.

She jumped to her feet when Bruce Kelly and Wyatt approached. One look at Wyatt's face and concern sliced through her. His complexion was ashen. Grayish circles rimmed his eyes, and his hair looked as though he'd run his hands through the thick strands a few times.

"Well?" She held her breath, not daring to assume anything.

"He passed," Bruce said. "He's free to go home."

Relief washed over her like a spring rain. It took every ounce of control she had to keep from launching herself at Wyatt and hugging him. He looked as if he needed a hug. But not from her. "Come on, cowboy, let's get you home to Gabby. She needs her daddy."

Wyatt gave her a tired, grateful smile. "Thanks."

The temperature outside had dropped considerably. She zipped up her jacket as they walked across the parking lot to her SUV. She was sharply aware of him as he followed her to the driver's side. She tucked in her chin and titled her head to look into his eyes. The light from the parking-lot lamp cast shadows over the planes and angles of his face. "Yes?"

"Mind if I drive? I'm too antsy to be a passenger."

She understood. His life was careening out of control. Driving at least gave him some semblance of power over his destiny. She pressed the keys into his hand. "Here you go."

He curled his fingers over hers and kept her in place. "Why did you come to the station?"

The gentle pressure of his skin touching hers was making it hard to concentrate on the question. Why indeed? "I made a promise to my aunt and uncle that I'd make sure the investigation was done fairly."

"Isn't that what Mr. Kelly's for?"

He had her there. Without a good answer, she shrugged and slipped past him to move around the back of the vehicle toward the passenger side. He came around the front and met her at the door, which he opened for her. "My lady."

Her heart did a funny little jump that made her insides all soft and squishy. She shouldn't care, but she liked his gentlemanly manners. More often than not, she was the one opening car doors to hustle a client inside a vehicle. Not having to do so made her feel feminine, cared for—things she wasn't used to feeling.

Attraction zipped along her nerve endings and almost made her forget her vow to never, ever again get involved with someone she worked with, including the person she was protecting.

Even if Wyatt wasn't technically her client.

But getting involved with him would only complicate the situation, not to mention put her heart at risk of being decimated. She knew what that felt like. She didn't want to feel that way again.

Why did she find herself attracted to men who were off-limits?

Granted, the limits were self-imposed, but still…

She blew out a sharp breath. She couldn't forget what Trent had told her.

You are not trying to prove his innocence. Or guilt. You are not his bodyguard.

Better stop thinking of Wyatt as anything other than her aunt and uncle's employer. She had to get control of the ridiculous way she reacted to his mere presence.

A hard feat, considering he sat only a few inches from

her. His every move distracted her. He placed his Stetson on the seat between them as if to put up a physical barrier. Better able to think when not looking at him, she forced herself to pay attention to the road ahead as Wyatt drove sedately out of town. He sped up on the long stretch of highway leading to the ranch.

Darkness had quietly claimed the land, covering the pastures she knew stretched out along either side of the road. Against the night sky, the silhouette of the Snowy Range Mountains was visible.

Stars twinkled in the heavens. A clear, cold night. A beautiful night.

Yet Jackie couldn't appreciate the beauty when her mind was churning with all that had happened, despite her best intentions not to think about it. There was a murder to solve in order to clear Wyatt's name. Problem was, she wasn't sure where to look. Someone had warned George to keep his mouth shut. But why? What had George known that had been worth killing him for? Who wrote the note? And who had led him to his death?

Was there a connection between the mining company and George's death?

If she were working this case, she'd do a thorough background check into Degas Corporation and their representative, Richard Pendleton.

But she wasn't working this case. Or any case. Those days were long gone.

She really needed to return to Boston. Get back to her life.

Wyatt had his lawyer. He'd passed the polygraph, and though the test did not conclusively prove his innocence, it did open up the possibly that someone other than Wyatt was guilty. The sheriff and the state investigator would have to start looking elsewhere for George's murderer.

There was no reason for Jackie to remain in Wyoming.

At the mailboxes, Wyatt turned onto the road that would take them home.

Jackie gave herself a mental shake. Not her home. Wyatt's.

A deafening noise jarred Jackie, setting her senses on alert. The SUV vibrated and swerved into a skid. They'd blown a tire.

"Hold on!" Wyatt yelled as he struggled to maintain control of the vehicle. The skid became a spin on the snow-packed road. The world flashed by in swirling shades of darkness, reminding her of a carnival tilt-a-whirl.

She braced herself with her left hand on the dashboard and the other on the door. "Lord, please protect us," she breathed out.

The front end of the truck slammed into a deep V on the side of the road.

Wyatt put his arm out to save her as the impact flung her forward. The air bag deployed, jamming her arm into her shoulder socket and slamming into her face and chest. Pain exploded through her from multiple points of contact. Her skin burned and stung at the same time. Just as quickly as the air bag inflated, it deflated. A horrible chemical smell filled the cab of the truck. She choked on a cough before catching her breath.

With a groan, she righted herself, wincing as she

moved her left arm. Something sticky trickled down her forehead.

Wyatt was slumped forward over the steering wheel, the deflated ends of the air bag sticking out from beneath him.

Fear spurted through her. "Wyatt!"

She nudged him. Nothing.

Her heart contracted painfully in her chest. "Please, Lord, don't let him be dead."

Wyatt groaned as sensations assaulted him all at once. His face hurt. His ribs throbbed. Gravity pinned his body forward over the steering wheel. The seat belt dug painfully across his chest, and an acrid smell burned his nostrils.

"Wyatt, come on. Wake up. That's it."

Jackie's voice drew him fully awake. He opened his eyes and found himself staring out the front window at dirt and snow lit up by the truck's headlights.

In a flash, he remembered the bang of the tire blowing and the truck sliding and then spinning right into a ditch. He turned his head and winced. Sharp pain jabbing behind his eyes made sweat break out on his brow.

He forced himself to stay focused and sucked in a breath at the sight of Jackie next to him. Blood dripped from a gash on her forehead, red abrasions covered her pretty face and her wide blue eyes were clouded with pain.

"You're hurt." He coughed as his lungs seized from breathing in the chemical agent released with the air bag.

"Yeah. My shoulder hurts like crazy," she said, holding her left arm tight to her body.

He pushed himself back, bracing a hand on the steering wheel as he reached for his cell phone to call for help.

The back window exploded in a spray of glass.

A bullet slammed into the radio.

"Down!" Jackie yelled and reached out to pull him from the line of sight.

Ducking, he worked to free his seat belt. "I didn't hear the shot."

"Suppressor" came her terse reply. "Help me with my belt."

Once he was free of the seat belt, he worked at unclasping hers. She immediately slid to the floor. Wyatt lay across the seat.

"We have to get out of here," Jackie said, "or we're as good as dead."

His heart rate ratcheted up even more. Unfortunately, they couldn't drive away because the front end of the SUV was nose down in a ditch. He didn't like how vulnerable they were.

She shimmied around so she could reach the door handle. Planting her feet on the door, she gave it a hard shove. It bounced open on its hinges and slammed back shut.

More bullets riddled the truck.

One image formed in his head. Gabby. No way would he leave her an orphan.

Wyatt scooted closer to the door, and together they got it open. Jackie scrambled out; Wyatt followed headfirst, using his arms for support. He tumbled into the deep ravine packed with snow, rocks and debris from the road, righted himself and crouched, ignoring the painful ache in his ribs. He got his phone out and dialed the sheriff's department.

After quickly explaining the situation to Eleanor, the dispatcher, he hung up. "Help's on the way."

Grimly, Jackie held a gun in her right hand. "Keep your head down."

Purpose hardened on her pretty face. She was a bodyguard. A woman intent on keeping him alive. He hoped she didn't get any more hurt in the process.

She made her way to the back of the truck and crawled up the lip of the ditch to peer out at the expanse of pasture on the other side of the road.

The spit of dirt flying sent a jolt of fear through Wyatt. The bullets came too close to Jackie. She dived to the side and scrambled around the truck. She hissed in pain and clutched at her left arm, but the determination on her face never wavered.

She crouched beside him. "Whoever's shooting at us is positioned out in that field. I'm betting he's got a powerful scope and a tactical rifle."

"How can you tell?"

"I can't for sure. But it's what I'd have if I were out there," she replied, her breath coming out in a visible puff against the cold air.

Disturbed by the thought of her as a sniper, he asked, "What do we do now?"

"Hope he stays put while we wait for the sheriff," she said.

Wyatt didn't want to sit on his hands. *He* wouldn't stay put if he were a sniper. He wanted to find out who was trying to kill them. "Shouldn't we do something?

"Negative. We're safer here using the truck as cover and waiting for the cavalry."

"Isn't it your job to go after the bad guy?"

"In another line of work, but now my job is to protect you," she said, moving so she could see over the top of the ditch. He grabbed a handful of her jacket, ready to yank her out of harm's way.

They heard an engine turn over. Jackie tensed beneath his hand. Wyatt strained to listen. The rev of the engine was not a car or motorcycle, but the purr of a snowmobile.

And it was drawing closer.

"Come on," Jackie urged. "We have to find better cover."

"There's nowhere to go," Wyatt said grimly, staring out at the inky shadows of the flat pastureland on the other side of the road.

"We need to get away from the truck." She gestured for him to follow her. "We can use the darkness as cover and pray this guy doesn't have night-vision goggles."

Though he trusted she knew what she was doing, he sent up a quick plea. *Okay, God, we need You now.*

In a low crouch, they ran along the ditch away from the truck, letting the darkness swallow them. They had made it about four yards when the snowmobile came into view. Jackie pulled Wyatt down to a prone position in the ditch. The lone gunman wore all white, including a face mask. He held a big rifle in his hands.

And there was no doubt in Wyatt's mind they'd be dead if Jackie hadn't thought quickly and hustled them away from the truck.

Wyatt heard the man swear, and then he quickly swung his gaze around.

Instinctively, Wyatt lowered his head to the ground, afraid the man would see the whites of his eyes.

The sound of sirens fast approaching sent the gun-toting man on the snowmobile zooming back the way he'd come.

Wyatt breathed a sigh of relief just as Jackie moaned and pushed herself to a seated position. She'd saved his life; now it was his turn to help her. He slid his arm around her waist. She started in surprise and then leaned into him as they made their way back to the truck.

Headlights and flashing reds and blues cut through the night and illuminated the back end of the black SUV sticking up in the air.

The sheriff's car skidded to a halt. Another sheriff's department vehicle and an ambulance ground to a stop next to the sheriff's car.

Landers jumped out of his vehicle. "Wyatt!"

"Here," Wyatt answered, surprised by how glad he was to see his stepfather. It wasn't Landers per se, Wyatt rationalized—he'd feel the same about anyone who'd arrived right about now.

Landers rushed to meet them. A fierce frown wrinkled his brow. "Either of you hit?"

"No. A little banged up from the crash," Wyatt said.

"A guy on a snowmobile went that way," Jackie said, gesturing with her uninjured arm. "He took position about three hundred yards out in the pasture. You should check for shell casings."

Landers nodded and helped her out of the ditch. "I'll

put my deputies on it, but let's concentrate on getting you two to the hospital."

Two paramedics wearing matching navy slacks and thick jackets rushed up. Wyatt relinquished Jackie to the care of the female EMT. She led Jackie over to the open bay of the ambulance where she cleaned her gash, while the other paramedic shone a penlight in Wyatt's eyes.

He waved him off. "I'm fine, Jake."

"You've got a nasty-looking bruise on your forehead, and I'd imagine your ribs took a hard blow from the air bag," Jake replied.

"It's not that bad," Wyatt ground out. He'd suffered broken ribs before. This pain wasn't as bad as then.

"Let me do my job, Wyatt."

Forcing himself to submit to Jake's ministration, Wyatt watched Landers giving orders to two deputies. The two men took off toward where Jackie had said the shooter had been positioned. Their flashlights bobbed in the dark, marking their progress.

Landers approached and stopped near Wyatt. "Tell me what happened."

"The tire blew, and we went into the ditch. Next thing I know we're taking fire," Wyatt said.

Without comment, Landers went to the truck to inspect the tire.

Wyatt sucked in a breath when Jake pressed his hand against Wyatt's side.

"I don't think you've broken any ribs," Jake said. "But to be on the safe side, I want you to go to the hospital and have an X-ray taken."

"I don't think that's necessary," Wyatt replied. "I need to get home." He worried for his daughter's safety.

Would whoever had shot at him try to hurt him through Gabby?

"You took a bad thump on the head, Wyatt. You could have internal bleeding, or at the least a concussion. You need to go to the hospital."

"Wyatt, go with Ms. Blain to the hospital," Landers said as he returned. "If not for your sake, then for hers."

Following the sheriff's gaze, Wyatt looked at Jackie. She had a white bandage wrapped around her head, and her left arm was in a sling. Seeing her injured, he felt a knot of anxiety and anger in his chest. That she was hurt because of him ripped him up inside.

The last thing he ever wanted was to hurt another woman.

Jackie in particular. She'd been kind to him and Gabby. She didn't deserve to be knee-deep in this mess. As soon as possible, he was going to send her on her way. Better for her sake to leave before anything else happened to her.

She climbed into the back of the ambulance and met his gaze. Her eyebrow arched, and she patted the seat next to her on the gurney.

The need to be with her rose sharply, catching him off guard. He was powerless to refuse.

"I'll go. Let me check in with Carl first," Wyatt said, pressing the speed-dial number for Carl's cell. He had to know that Gabby was safe.

When Carl answered, he was horrified to hear what had happened and assured Wyatt that all was well at the ranch. For now, Wyatt thought, but for how long?

"Sheriff, can you have a deputy drive out and keep watch over Gabby and the Kirks?"

"Done," Landers replied.

Satisfied he didn't have to worry about Gabby, he ambled over to the ambulance and climbed in next to Jackie.

"I hate hospitals," she whispered and folded her hand around his.

Cradling her hand felt natural, right. Her bones were delicate and her skin soft. Absently, his thumb stroked hers. He realized what he was doing and quickly stopped.

"Have ever since I was a kid. I went to visit my grandfather before he died from emphysema." She shuddered. "The smells and sounds gave me nightmares."

"I'll be with you," he said, touched by her vulnerability. His chest expanded with tenderness usually reserved for his daughter, only this was different. There was nothing paternal about the affection and attraction zinging through his blood, wrapping around his heart.

"Whew," she said and leaned her head against his shoulder. Every nerve ending in his body jumped as though he'd been zapped by a live wire. "Whatever they gave me is working."

His stomach muscles clenched. He nearly groaned aloud with disgust at himself. *Get a grip, Monroe. She has drugs in her system.* If she didn't, she wouldn't be cuddling so close. Jackie was nothing if not professional. And he better keep himself in check. She needed him to be strong and in control.

But he couldn't deny how good it felt to be needed by her. Even if it was only to get her through a visit to the hospital.

He'd have to make sure he didn't get too used to the

good feelings, because once she was back to her normal, adorable and independent self, she wouldn't need him. No matter how much a tiny part of him wished she would.

EIGHT

As she lay in the E.R. on an exam table behind a drawn curtain, Jackie shook her head, trying to dispel the fuzzy-headedness clouding her mind. The doctor had just left her with instructions to rest. As if she could do that when she didn't know where Wyatt was. She should be protecting him, making sure the bad guys out to get him weren't closing in. She may not have started this journey as his bodyguard, but now it was clear he needed one. Purpose slid into place.

She pushed herself to a sitting position.

Oh, not a good idea. Her head pounded. She winced and felt the biting sting of the stitches in her forehead. The doctor had said the sutures were small and wouldn't leave a scar.

That was good, she guessed. Not that she cared. Worrying about her looks wasn't high on her list of priorities. Her capabilities as a bodyguard weren't dependent on a pretty face. In fact, her looks worked against her at times. People seemed hard-pressed to take her seriously. But then again, being underestimated tended to work in her favor in some situations.

Swinging her feet off the bed, she stood and steadied

herself with her uninjured hand. Her left arm was in a sling, held tightly against her body. When the air bag had deployed, the force rammed her humerus bone into her shoulder socket, causing traumatic impingement. Thankfully nothing was broken, though it would be a matter of time to see how she healed. The doc had said if persistent pain occurred, then it could mean she had a torn tendon, which could require surgery.

She did not want surgery. It was bad enough having a sore shoulder. It would make protecting Wyatt that much harder, but she'd manage. *Please, Lord, heal my shoulder quickly.*

The curtain parted, sending a jolt to her heart.

Wyatt and Sheriff Landers crowded in.

Glad to see Wyatt up and around and safe, she asked, "What did the doc say about your ribs?"

"Bruised. Not nearly as bad as when I took one of Alexander's hoofs in the side," Wyatt answered with a wry grin.

Her gaze snagged on the discoloration on his forehead. "And your head?"

"Hard."

"Doc says he's good to go home," Landers interjected.

She swayed. Wyatt rushed to grip her by her good elbow. "The doctor said you should be resting."

"I was coming to find you," she said, allowing him to help her back onto the exam table. Turning her attention to the sheriff, she asked, "What have you found out?"

Landers held up an evidence bag. The glare of the hospital exam room's overhead lights glinted off the brass shell casings inside the clear plastic. "We found six casings. I'll have our forensics expert identify the make and dust for prints."

Jackie squinted and studied the shell casings. "They're .308 rounds."

Landers nodded. "Used by hunters."

"And marksmen," she stated grimly. "Whoever was shooting at us wasn't some weekend warrior out hunting snipe."

"The tire didn't blow on its own," Landers said. "We found a slug embedded in the rubber."

Jackie met Wyatt's stunned gaze. "This has gone beyond trying to frame you for murder. Now we know you're being targeted, cowboy. Can you think of a reason why someone wants you dead?"

Wyatt ran a hand through his hair. "No. I mean, I've made a lot of people angry by not signing away the mineral rights to my property, but I can't imagine someone would resort to murder over it."

Jackie scoffed. "You'd be surprised what people will do when it comes to money."

He frowned and shook his head. "I guess."

"Who benefits if you die?" Jackie pressed. "Who's the beneficiary to your estate?"

Wyatt's gaze transferred to his stepfather. "My mother and Gabby."

Sheriff Landers's eyebrows shot up. "I didn't know that. Gabby inheriting the ranch stands to reason. But does your mother know?"

"No. I had my will changed after Dina died."

"Was Dina the sole beneficiary before her death?" Landers asked.

"She was until Gabby was born. Then I added Gabby."

Jackie had to wonder if whoever was targeting Wyatt thought that with him out of the way they could gain control of the estate once Gabby inherited the ranch. "Do you have guardians in place in case something happens to you?"

Wyatt's gaze bore into her. "Your aunt and uncle."

Well, that shot one theory out the window. Her aunt and uncle wouldn't hurt Wyatt or Gabby.

The sound of an old-fashioned phone ringing came from the sheriff's pocket. "Excuse me," he said and stepped out of the curtain to answer.

Wyatt's own cell phone chirped. He looked at the phone and answered. "Carl? What's wrong?"

Fear flashed in Wyatt's dark eyes. Jackie sucked in a tense breath as she waited. Her heart sped up.

"I'll be right there," Wyatt said tersely and hung up. "The ranch—"

Landers rushed back in. "Wyatt, the ranch is on fire."

Red-and-orange flames licked the walls of the feed shed, consuming the wooden structure and grains inside. The glow illuminated the night so brightly that Wyatt could see it when they were still a mile out. Shadows danced over the fire truck and firemen working to douse the blaze. Stomach tied in a knot, Wyatt didn't give a fig about the shed; his only concern was for the people he loved—Gabby and the Kirks and the brave men and women who'd rushed to their aid. He sent a plea of safety heavenward and was thankful to see the three people dearest to him huddled near the untouched porch of the house.

As soon as the sheriff's car rolled to a halt, Wyatt jumped out the passenger door and ran to his daughter.

"Daddy!" Gabby launched herself from Carl's hold to Wyatt's arms.

His chest tightened as he hugged her close, breathing in the scent of her baby shampoo. Tears of relief burned the back of his eyes. Over her head, he asked Carl, "What happened?"

"Don't rightly know," Carl replied, his weathered face pale in the glow from the fire. "We heard this bang and then a *whoosh*. Next thing I know the shed's engulfed in flames."

"Jackie!" Penny exclaimed and ran down the stairs to meet Jackie as she climbed from the sheriff's vehicle.

Wyatt met Jackie's gaze. By tacit agreement they had kept the details to themselves. No sense in upsetting the others right now with talk of a sniper on a snowmobile.

Wyatt's heart pitched. Jackie looked battered and beautiful. A white bandage covered the stitched gash on her forehead, and her left arm hugged her body in a navy sling. Her loose blond curls framed her face and spilled down her back. Her blue eyes reflected the gold of the fire. His heart twisted. They'd come close to dying tonight.

Now someone had set fire to the feed shed. Whatever was going on had escalated. Someone not only wanted Wyatt dead, but they also wanted to damage the ranch. He stroked his daughter's hair and took in the smoldering mess on his land. Thankfully, the house hadn't been set on fire.

A shiver of dread worked its way through him. No telling what the person might do next time. He hugged

Gabby tightly. He would have to make sure there wasn't a next time.

Landers approached. "The fire chief says they've got the blaze under control. Once it's completely out, they'll be able to determine the cause."

"I'm glad the fire didn't jump to the stables," Carl stated grimly. "Just to be safe, I moved the horses to the corral."

The thought of the animals suffering lodged fear the size of a fist in his chest. "Good thinking."

The noise of the shed collapsing drew their attention. The structure folded in on itself, and the flames lessened as the fire hoses soaked the smoldering wood. Soon only smoke rising in wisps from the charred remains was visible through the glare of the fire-truck headlights.

The fire chief walked over. He was a big man with a bald head, shiny with sweat and streaked with soot. "In the morning we'll do our inspection. But as hot as this fire burned, I'd say definitely arson. The back of the shed burned hotter and faster, suggesting the point of origin. Most likely an accelerant was used."

No surprise there. But why? What did anyone gain from burning down the feed shed? What did anyone gain by shooting at him and Jackie?

After the fire trucks and Landers left, Wyatt took Gabby inside and put her to bed. Jackie went with her aunt and uncle to their dwelling. They agreed to meet up in the morning to hear the official cause of the fire.

"Daddy, stay with me. I'm scared," Gabby said as he tucked the pink comforter around her small body. Her green eyes appeared watery with unshed tears in the warm glow of the night-light plugged into the wall at her bedside.

Hating to see her distress, he lay down beside her on top of the blankets, mindful that his clothes were dirty. But washing the comforter was a small price to pay to ease his daughter's mind. "I'm here, sweetie. I'm not going to let anything happen to you."

Saying the words aloud made his stomach churn. How could he protect his family from a threat he didn't understand?

She sighed and turned on her side, hugging a stuffed rabbit. "I love you, Daddy."

He stroked her red curls. His chest expanded with emotion. "I love you, sweetie."

She was his world, the best thing that had come out of his marriage. A gift from God that humbled him every day.

He didn't deserve Gabby, didn't deserve her sweet innocence in his life. But for whatever reason, God had deemed him fit to parent this little girl.

He prayed daily that God would help him be the father he should be.

Inadequacy surged through him. The parental example he'd had wasn't one he wanted to emulate. Even before his mother left them, Emerson Monroe had been a drunk.

Usually not mean, but definitely not attentive or interested in raising the son who so desperately wanted his father's attention. The painful memories of trying to gain his father's approval hung like stones around Wyatt's neck, reminding him daily not to become his father. Wyatt would make sure his child knew she was loved every moment of every day. She had to know that nothing she did would ever make him stop loving her.

And he would protect her with his dying breath.

Which it seemed someone was bent on taking from him.

He let his eyes drift closed as words rose to his lips. "Lord, please put a hedge of protection around us and keep us from harm. Keep Gabby safe. I know you see everything, Lord. Please show me who's doing this and why. Show me what I need to know to keep us safe."

The creak of a floorboard jerked him to full alert.

Someone was in the downstairs hall. A spot on the flooring had warped and needed to be replaced. He hadn't gotten around to fixing it. Now the squeaky board could be the thing that saved his life.

He jumped from the bed, ripped the covers back and scooped Gabby up into his arms. She let out a soft cry.

"Shh," he said. "It's okay. I need you to be very quiet."

Fear widened her green eyes, and her hands clutched his shirt.

He crossed to the closet, opened the door and, with his booted foot, kicked aside the toys. He set Gabby on the floor.

"Daddy?" she whispered, clinging to her stuffed rabbit.

He needed to make sure she remained safe. The closet was the only choice he had for a hiding place. Hating that he was scaring her, he said, "Stay here. I'll be right back."

He couldn't leave her in the dark, so he yanked on the chain for the overhead light. The closet filled with a soft glow. He closed the door.

He stilled, listening.

Where was the person? He imagined a man dressed in white from head to toe creeping up the stairs, along the carpeted hall toward the room. He could envision the lethal weapon in his hands.

No doubt it would have a silencer—or suppressor, as Jackie called it. Whatever. No one would hear the shots. He and Gabby would be dead, the killer long gone before anyone realized something was wrong.

Wyatt couldn't let that happen.

He searched the room for a weapon he could use. Nothing but stuffed animals, dolls, books and puzzles. A tea set. What he wouldn't give for the bat that was in the downstairs hall closet.

His gaze landed on the beautiful porcelain unicorn sitting in a place of honor on top of Gabby's dresser. The figurine had been a gift from George. Wyatt had put it up high because he'd been afraid Gabby would hurt herself on the pointy gold tip of the unicorn's horn.

For a fleeting moment he contemplated using the knickknack. He could smash it against the person's head when he entered.

But that would require crossing the room in front of the door, and his instincts told him he didn't have time. The slight creak of the floorboards in front of the door confirmed his thought.

His best bet was to tackle the intruder and hope he could gain control of the gun.

NINE

Wyatt positioned himself near the hinges of Gabby's bedroom door seconds before it slowly swung open.

Muscles tense, breath turning shallow, he readied himself, preparing to launch an assault on the invading enemy the moment he appeared in his line of sight.

"Wyatt?"

Jackie's voice jolted through him like the electric shock he'd had as a kid when he'd stuck a fork in a socket just to see if the warning of danger his mother had given was real.

He gripped the edge of the door and pulled it wide, needing to prove to himself Jackie was truly here and not some figment of his imagination.

She started, stepping back into a fighting stance, her right arm coming up as if to ward off an attack. At her feet stood her dog, Spencer. The English bulldog panted as if the exertion from climbing the stairs had taken its toll.

Relief and anger and then more relief flooded Wyatt until he thought he'd drown with the choking sensation squeezing his lungs. "What are you doing? You scared me spitless," he managed to get out past the constriction in his throat.

"Sorry. I came over to check on you," she said, relaxing her stance. "You shouldn't leave the front door unlocked."

The chastisement hit him in the solar plexus. He'd been careless, in too much of a hurry to get Gabby upstairs, and hadn't taken the necessary safeguards.

He'd never had to worry about locking the doors. The ranch was so far from town, so private; he'd always felt safe, protected.

But that illusion was shattered now. Should have crumbled the moment he found George's dead body on his porch. Even then, he hadn't let the full implications of the murder sink in. Now he realized how vulnerable they were out here so far away from town.

Hadn't he just asked God to show him how to keep Gabby safe?

Jackie coming inside his house uninvited and undetected was an effective way of slamming home the need for caution. He wouldn't be making that mistake again.

He turned and retrieved Gabby from the closet. Tears streaked down her face as she clung to his neck. He soothed her with soft words and tender strokes down her back. Her body trembled in his arms.

He sat on the bed with her in his lap. He wasn't sure his legs could hold them up anymore. He was emotionally spent.

"Hey, sweetie," Jackie said, crouching beside them and brushing back a damp curl from Gabby's face. "I didn't mean to scare you and your daddy."

"Someone burned the feed shed," Gabby said, her voice tiny.

Jackie's lips twisted. "Yes, they did."

"A bad man," Gabby said.

Surprise jarred Wyatt. "Did you see the man?"

Gabby nodded. "From the window."

Wyatt met Jackie's gaze. Fury darkened her blue eyes.

"Can you tell us what he looked like?" Jackie asked, her voice gentle.

"Did you recognize the man?" Wyatt asked.

Gabby's gaze bounced between them. "I thought it was Daddy at first. But Daddy wouldn't burn down the shed."

That rocked Wyatt back on his heels. The same man who'd led George to his death?

Jackie touched Gabby's knee. "You're right, it wasn't your daddy. But you don't have to worry. Your daddy and I won't let the bad man come near you."

Gabby tightened her hold on him. His heart squeezed all on its own.

"Hey, I have an idea," Jackie said. "How about Spencer sleeps in your room tonight? He's a good watchdog."

Wyatt's gaze slid to the dog lying in the middle of the room with his paws beneath his chin, his pink tongue hanging out the side of his mouth. Yeah, Wyatt could picture the dog taking someone down. Not.

"Really?" Gabby said. "Can he, Daddy? Can he sleep with me?"

Unable to deny her anything at the moment, he said, "He can stay in the room, but he's not to come on the bed."

"Awww, Daddy," Gabby complained.

"Your Daddy's right. Spencer stays on the floor but he'll sleep right by the bed."

Gabby scrambled off his lap and dived under the covers. Pulling the comforter to her chin, she said, "You can go now, Daddy. Spencer and I will be okay."

Shaking his head, Wyatt leaned over and placed a kiss on Gabby's forehead. "Okay, sweetie. Good night."

"Night, Daddy," she said. "Night, Jackie."

Jackie smiled softly. "Good night, little princess."

Wyatt's heart squeezed tight at the affection in Jackie's eyes. The tender expression on her pretty face made her even more appealing. What would it be like to have her look at him with such tenderness?

Attraction slammed into him with the force of a physical blow. She'd changed her clothes. She now wore soft-looking sweatpants in bright purple and a matching zip-up jacket. The white square on her forehead and the sling holding her left arm against her body were stark reminders of the trauma they'd suffered. Her blond curls were damp and clipped up. She smelled fresh, like springtime.

Tempering his reaction, he slipped from the bed and crossed to the door.

He couldn't forget that someone had come onto his land and started a fire. Someone resembling him. Just like the person who led George away from the saloon. His fingers curled into tight fists.

With a few spoken commands from Jackie, Spencer got up and moved to the side of the bed. He plopped down with a soft *oaf.*

Gabby hung over the side of the bed to pet him.

Jackie joined Wyatt at the door, her soft blue gaze going to Gabby. "She's so sweet."

"Yes." Though his gaze stayed on the woman in front of him. She was sweet, too. Sweet and kind. Brave and capable.

She drew him into the hall. He closed Gabby's door behind him.

"I'm going to stay here tonight," Jackie said, her tone firm. "To make sure nothing happens to you two."

He blinked. His mouth went dry. "Here?"

She nodded. "Yes. I'll stand guard downstairs."

His mind grappled with her words. She was going to stay in his house, downstairs, standing guard while... what? She expected him to sleep? Not when there was someone out there threatening both his life and his daughter's.

"I appreciate your willingness to stay, but I can protect Gabby."

"It's what I do."

"You're injured," he pointed out. "I won't let you put yourself in any more danger or risk being hurt again."

"You needn't worry about me. It's you who's in danger," she countered. "I don't need my left hand to shoot."

He hoped she wouldn't have to shoot at all. The very thought of it filled him with dread.

"Besides," she continued, "my shoulder's not that bad. I've had cracked ribs that have hurt worse."

He hated to think how or why she'd had her ribs cracked. "You need to rest."

"So do you."

Frustration gripped him. "You don't need to stay here. I'm sure your aunt and uncle want you at their house."

"I've already talked to them. They agree that the best place for me tonight is here. That's why they called me in the first place. To protect you. You and Gabby."

His heart hammered against his bruised ribs. "I'm not comfortable with you here."

She arched an eyebrow. "Why?"

Short of admitting he was attracted to her and that having her close at hand wouldn't bring him any sort of peace, he wasn't sure what to say. There was no reason not to accept her offer of protection tonight.

His ego wanted to refuse, to say he didn't need her. He wanted to be the one she turned to for protection, not the other way around.

But then again, his daughter's safety was at stake.

If it were only him, he would send Jackie on her way before he gave in to the temptation to pull her close and kiss her.

For Gabby, he'd control his emotions and be grateful for the extra security. "Fine. You can stay tonight. But I'll stand guard with you."

One corner of her mouth lifted. "Of course you will."

Confused by that remark, he asked, "What does that mean?"

She laid her hand on his chest, her palm creating a warm spot over his heart. "It means you're a good father and a smart man."

Capturing her hand, he couldn't resist lifting her knuckles to his lips. "Thank you."

Her eyes widened and darkened with what he was sure was yearning. Her lips parted. A silent invitation?

His resolve to control the attraction arcing between

them teetered. Before he could totally lose it, she slipped her hand from his and stepped back.

"I call it like I see it, cowboy."

With that she walked away and disappeared down the stairs, leaving him to wonder just what she saw in him. Did he measure up, or was he found wanting?

Who was he kidding? Of course he'd been found wanting. Hadn't he learned his lesson with Dina? He wasn't husband material. Best to remember that before he lost his head—and his heart—to the pretty bodyguard.

Jackie settled on the couch with a cup of hot chocolate in her hands and faced a big-screen television positioned above a gas fireplace. Beside her on the leather cushion sat her weapon, a SIG Sauer at the ready. She'd already done a perimeter sweep, assuring herself that the house was locked up tight.

She'd also set several alerts, including smashing three lightbulbs and sprinkling the fine fragments on the porch near each door and beneath the windows. If anyone came close to the house, she'd hear them crunching on the glass. Even with the precaution, she still couldn't relax, despite the warmth and coziness of the living room.

Only the table lamp lent the space any light, the soft luminosity pooling in a circle that chased the shadows into the corners. Bookshelves lined the walls. A recliner sat off to the side of the couch. A coffee table cluttered with coloring books and crayons sat between the couch and the TV. Pictures of Gabby as a baby and toddler graced the walls.

Overhead, the pipes groaned as the shower turned on. Wyatt.

Staring into her mug of chocolate, she concentrated on the little marshmallows melting into pools of white to keep her mind off him. She was glad he felt safe enough to get cleaned up. She half expected him to forgo the shower and change of clothes in order to keep watch over his daughter. He probably would have if Jackie hadn't shown up. She was going to have to talk to him about installing a security system. And getting a dog. A big one with a big bark.

She'd been able to enter the house unimpeded. Wyatt was probably used to the privacy and security of being so far from civilization. But that serene illusion had been burned to ash tonight, just like the shed.

The destruction seemed pointless. Sure, Wyatt lost money on the feed and would have to rebuild the shed. But that couldn't be the only purpose behind the fire.

The attack on the road had been quite pointed.

The two events contrasted drastically, though.

The sniper had to have been a professional, a hired gun using a weapon no ordinary criminal would be able to obtain without a fat bankroll, whereas the fire in the shed was almost amateurish. Weird.

If someone had wanted to hurt Wyatt and cause real damage, why not burn down the barn housing his prized stallion—or the house? A warning, perhaps?

She sighed and set the mug on the coffee table. Too many unknowns, and the questions were driving her to distraction. Needing some action, some task to perform to keep her hands and mind centered on the danger at hand, she got up and double-checked all the windows and doors on the main floor.

She gazed out the side window at her aunt and uncle's house. The porch light glowed brightly, as did the living room lights. She doubted they'd get any sleep tonight, either. After she'd told them about the sniper taking out the truck and the man on the snowmobile, they'd been understandably upset. She'd promised them she'd be careful.

She'd also called Trent Associates. Her boss was concerned and offered to send help. But because this wasn't a paid assignment, she could hardly accept. She'd have to rely on the sheriff and his men for backup. But it was nice to know James Trent had her back if needed.

Besides, she could just imagine how Wyatt would react if a team of bodyguards descended on the ranch. She'd been hard-pressed to get him to agree to let her stay.

The creak of a floorboard near the stairs sent alarm spiraling down her spine. She pivoted, bringing her weapon up as she faced the threat.

"Whoa, it's only me." Wyatt stepped out of the shadows, his hands held up. The pale light from the moon shining through the window deepened the shadows on his face. He'd changed into soft-looking chinos and a long-sleeved thermal shirt. His hair was damp and pushed back from his face.

Lowering her gun, she let out the breath trapped in her lungs. "You move quietly for a big man."

One side of his mouth tipped up. "I can start stomping if it would make you feel better."

Tucking her weapon into the pocket of her jacket,

she shook her head. "You don't need to change on my account."

He cocked his head and held her gaze. "That's good to know."

Enthralled by the intensity flaring in his dark eyes, her nerve endings tingled. Something indefinable passed between them, as if her acceptance of him touched a painful place deep inside him. An answering ache throbbed in her bones.

Needing to retreat from the force of his concentration, she sought ought a neutral topic. "I made hot chocolate. Would you care for some?"

His left eyebrow arched. "Playing hostess, are we?"

Heat crept into her cheeks. Maybe she'd overstepped, but she hadn't thought he'd mind if she took the liberty of preparing beverages. "I'm sorry."

He chuckled. "No need to be sorry. I'll pass on the chocolate. I'm glad you feel at home here."

And she did feel at home. More so than her own apartment. There was something inexplicable about the way being in Wyatt's home wrapped around her like a warm blanket. She wasn't sure if it was the homeyness, or the fact that there was so much love between him and Gabby that it made the dwelling more than just walls and furniture. Contentment filled her. A sense of belonging tugged at her heart. She found herself relaxing in a way she never had with anyone else.

Relaxed, but not complacent.

She couldn't afford to let her guard down. Danger lurked somewhere outside the walls of the house, and she didn't know why or who or where the threat was coming from. But the threat had access to sniper rifles and scopes and enough know-how to demand serious attention.

Keeping Wyatt and his daughter safe had to take precedence over anything else.

Even her emotions.

That meant she had to stay alert and in tune to the world around her. And to do that, she needed some distance from the all-too-appealing cowboy.

Unfortunately, physical distance wasn't going to be possible. Especially when everything about him sent her senses reeling and made her feel more at home than ever.

Regaining her equilibrium, she slipped past Wyatt and moved into the living room, where she retook her seat on the couch. Sinking into the soft leather, she grounded herself in the moment.

She stuffed a throw pillow beneath her injured elbow for support. The mild pain medication she'd taken earlier had dulled the throbbing to an annoying level but one she could handle. She set her weapon on the cushion next to her with her uninjured hand.

Wyatt followed her, sitting on the opposite end of the couch. His long, lean legs stretched out in front of him. His gaze went to the gun lying on the couch and then flicked away. The distance between them seemed to widen.

She sighed, wishing things could be different—their lives were different, but they weren't. His was a life dedicated to his daughter, to the land. Hers was dedicated to protecting people. Her life was always on the move. Each assignment took her somewhere new. The landscape always changing. Protectees spinning through her life like a revolving door.

Only with Wyatt, she wanted the cycle to stop. She wanted to hear his opinions, learn about his dreams.

Things she shouldn't need to know in order to provide protection. Most protectees liked to keep their bodyguards at a distance.

"Seen but not intrusive" was the catchphrase.

Jackie sometimes had a hard time abiding by that rule. She liked to dive in and see what made people tick. Maybe it was her years in law enforcement that made her want to know the motivations, the psychology behind behaviors.

But on this assignment—and yes, she had to think of Wyatt and Gabby as an assignment if she hoped to maintain any sense of professionalism—digging into the psyche of her protectee could prove to be her undoing if she weren't careful.

Forming an attachment to the handsome cowboy and his adorable daughter would make leaving Wyoming difficult.

His close proximity created agitated flutters in her tummy. He took up so much space, yet he was agile and economical in his movements, whether sipping tea with his daughter or hefting hay bales or slipping out of the shadows.

She tried not to wonder what it would feel like to be held against his strong chest, enclosed in his warm embrace. Disconcerted by the train of her thoughts, she picked up the mug of cocoa, but the liquid inside had gone cold. She set the cup back down.

"What would you be doing right now if you weren't here?" Wyatt asked.

Jackie played the question over in her mind. What

would she be doing? "It would depend on whether I was on an assignment or not. If not, I'd be home with Spencer. Most likely training or catching up on my DVR shows."

"On a Friday night?"

Her gaze shot to his. "Friday's no different than any other day of the week. Well, except Sunday. I'd attend church Sunday morning."

"No special someone to take you out and treat you like a queen?"

"Is this small talk or are you flirting with me?"

Was he fishing to see if she was available? A delighted thrill raced through her. Why would he care? Her pulse sped up. And if he were flirting with her, what then?

TEN

Surprise flickered across his face. "Both, I guess."

A warm flush infused her cheeks. He was attracted to her, too. A heady sense of empowerment rushed through her. She fought to temper her responses. She was acting like a schoolgirl with her first crush. Crushing on Wyatt wasn't a good idea; doing so would only lead to emotional heartache.

"There's no one special in my life right now," she answered honestly. And she had no intention of changing that. Unless, someday...

"But there was?"

She'd let that slip, hadn't she? "Once. But it was a mistake." She made a face. "I fell for a coworker, a fellow deputy back when I was with the Atkins sheriff's department."

His expression softened. "Didn't work out, I take it."

"No, it didn't." She let out a scornful scoff. "He dumped me to marry the mayor's daughter. Apparently they'd been carrying on for a while behind my back." She hated that traces of bitterness still infused her tone. "Made working at the sheriff's department difficult. The department wasn't exactly crazy about the idea of a female deputy to begin with, so eventually I walked away."

His gaze assessed her. "But you didn't want to."

She sighed. "No, it wasn't what I wanted at the time." Then she smiled. "But it all worked out for the best, you know. God had a plan for me. There are so many scriptures I cling to whenever life seems chaotic and random. And each one tells me God's plan is better than any I could ever come up with."

He nodded. She wasn't sure if he was agreeing that God's plan was better or that her life worked out for the best.

"I landed at Trent Associates a few months later, and life's been great. I love what I do. And I'm good at my job." She met his dark-eyed gaze. "I'm just really careful not to get involved romantically with the people I work with. Or the people I protect."

Something flickered across his face. His lips twisted in a rueful way that she found curious. "A wise decision."

More like self-preservation. Time to refocus this conversation. "Tell me about Dina."

His head snapped to the side as if she'd struck him. "There's not much to tell."

Not about to let him wiggle out of telling his tale, she went for the heart of the matter. "Did you kill your wife?"

Wyatt didn't deserve the tenderness echoing in her tone as she prodded him to tell her what had happened. "I didn't murder my wife." Guilt sliced through him, making him add, "But I am responsible for her death."

"What happened?" she pressed, her gaze unwavering.

"She fell down the stairs and hit her head. The blow

was fatal." Even to his own ears, his voice sounded robotic, monotone. But he couldn't allow himself to let any inflection, any emotion betray the torment of that day because if he cracked, he didn't know if he'd be able to put himself back together. And he needed to, for Gabby.

"Did you push her?"

He sucked in a sharp breath and felt the pain of her words stab him just as deeply as when his own mother had asked the same question. "No."

"Okay. Good."

Startled by her decisive tone, he stared. "You believe me?"

She regarded him steadily. "Is there a reason I shouldn't?"

He worked his mouth—he didn't know how to answer that. Finally he said, "My own mother doesn't believe me."

"She doesn't believe you killed George."

Surprise rocketed through him. He'd assumed she would, because she had before.

Jackie's blue eyes darkened with compassion. "Why wouldn't she believe you about your wife?"

He wanted to bolt, to get away from her searching questions. Regret anchored him to the seat. "My marriage wasn't perfect. In fact, it was pretty rocky."

He didn't know why he was telling her this, but he couldn't seem to keep his mouth from moving, the words from slipping out. "Dina and I met in college. She was from Seattle. We both came from broken homes. We got married the day after we graduated, and I brought her home to the ranch."

Jackie frowned slightly with a puzzled look. "That

man at the library, the one named Boyd—is he related to her?"

Surprised by the change in subject, he shook his head. "No. Boyd's local like me."

"Neighbors?"

"Yes, the Dunns' property touches the back acres of the Monroe ranch. Why?"

"Just curious." She smoothed a hand over the leather armrest next to her. "Moving to the ranch must have been a big adjustment for a city girl."

He drew in a breath and let it out. "It was. Being married was an adjustment for both of us. At first it was fun, new, different. But as time went on, she started to resent the isolation of the ranch and my dedication to it. We'd fight. Horrible fights, lots of yelling and slamming doors. She'd leave and go to my mother's. Of course, Mom knew me. She knew I had a temper."

"I can imagine you had some anger issues growing up," she commented. "With your dad's drinking and all."

He searched her face, looking for some sign of judgment, but her expression remained neutral as if they were discussing the weather rather than the intricacies of his personal life. A sense of relief crept in, but he couldn't trust the feeling. She'd been trained as a police officer. Part of the training had to include not allowing visible reactions. "Yeah, you could say that."

"It still doesn't make sense to me that your mother would think you would harm Dina." Jackie's gaze narrowed slightly. "Unless…"

"I never raised a hand to her," he said flatly. "Ever."

"But you were a hothead, and they worried you would lose control."

She'd nailed it. She seemed to read him so easily. He'd better remember to keep his guard up around her. "And when she died, they all assumed..."

"That you were at fault." She finished his thought. "That you'd finally snapped."

"Yes." He gave a dry laugh. "I'm sure Landers was itching to put me behind bars."

"If Sheriff Landers had been able to prove you were guilty of a crime, you'd be in jail and we wouldn't be having this conversation. Regardless of his feelings for you, the sheriff would do his job."

Wyatt snorted. "If he had his way, he'd lock me up now so fast it would make your head spin."

She arched an eyebrow. "You really believe that?"

"We don't exactly get along."

"Because you're too stubborn to see the truth," she remarked drily.

"Excuse me?"

"The sheriff cares about you."

He scoffed. "How could you even know that?"

"I've watched the way he has tried to protect you while still maintaining his professionalism. I'm sure he was the same then as now."

"You don't know what you're talking about." Landers had ridden him hard as a kid and teen, always on his case about his behavior, his attitude. The man had never once shown Wyatt affection or approval. Still didn't. Not that Wyatt gave the man the opportunity now. He'd spoken to Landers more in the past few days than he had in the past few years.

Every Sunday his mother and Landers took Gabby

for the afternoon. Wyatt never joined them, despite the fact that they invited him for dinner every time.

She lifted a slim shoulder. "I know what I see. And obviously there wasn't evidence of guilt. So how did she fall?"

"She tripped over one of Gabby's toys."

He could see Jackie's mind working as she held his gaze. Sitting so close, the specks of gold in her blue eyes were more visible. So pretty. His gaze caressed her face, touching on the defined cheekbones, the slight upward tilt to her slim nose and finally resting on her lush mouth.

Awareness shimmered down his spine and his blood stirred, pushing back all thought except for the woman seated next to him. The sharp longing to pull her close caught him off guard. His fingers curled around the edges of a throw pillow.

"There's more, though, isn't there?" she finally asked, forcing his gaze back to her eyes. "Something you're holding back."

His mouth turned to cotton. His heart hammered in his chest. How did she do that? Work her way under his carefully guarded walls?

The need to tell his story, to relate the events of that night, built in his midsection like the pressure inside a soda can threatening to explode from the tightly concealed container deep in his psyche where he'd stuffed all his memories, his guilt, his hurt. He didn't want to open up. He didn't deserve to be relieved of his burden of guilt.

She laid her hand over his. Her palm was soft but strong as she used gentle pressure to pry his hand away from the pillow. She held on to it, offering comfort he didn't deserve, couldn't accept. Yet he was powerless to pull away. Instead he clung to her like a lifeline in a storm-swept sea.

Words choked him, pushing past his resistance and forcing their way out. "We were arguing again," he confessed for the first time. "She was unhappy. Accusing me of not loving her enough."

Self-reproach twisted beneath his ribs. He'd loved Dina with as much of his heart as he could. But it hadn't been enough. Not for her. "She was so out of control. I kept telling her to be quiet. I was afraid Gabby would wake up and be scared. But Dina wouldn't stop yelling. Saying horrible things. Hurtful things."

The words rang in his mind now as clearly as that night. He forced those hateful words back into the cage deep inside. Not even for Jackie would he repeat Dina's words, no matter how good it felt to finally tell someone about that night.

"I knew I had to get out of there or I would lose it." He took a shuddering breath as the memories assaulted him. "I stormed out of our bedroom and down the stairs. She ran after me but tripped at the top of the stairs on Gabby's wooden train."

He closed his eyes, reliving that moment. "I heard her scream. Saw her tumble down the stairs."

He opened his eyes as he met Jackie's gaze. "She landed with a sickening thud on the hardwood floor. The force of the fall split her scalp. There was so much blood." The image of the dark stain pooling beneath her head was imprinted on his brain.

Jackie's gaze was on the staircase, as if she could see

the images in his mind. "And because you were argu-ing, everyone came to the conclusion that you were re-sponsible for her death."

He grimaced. "Not exactly. I never told anyone we were fighting that night."

Her gaze whipped to meet his. "Why not?"

"Because of exactly what you just said. If I'd told anyone we were in the middle of a quarrel when she fell, people would automatically assume I'd pushed her."

"But they came to that conclusion anyway."

The irony was not lost on him. "Yes, they did. I tried to revive her. And in the process, I contaminated the scene and transferred her blood to my clothes."

"As anyone would have. But it was an accident, so why do you blame yourself?"

"If we hadn't been arguing, if I'd kicked that train aside instead of stepping over it, if I'd been a better husband—loved her enough—she wouldn't have died. Gabby wouldn't be growing up without a mother."

"It takes two to argue. And two to make a marriage work."

Wise words. "In theory."

"In truth," she said, her voice adamant. "My parents have been married for nearly forty years. They would be the first to say it's hard work keeping a marriage going, but it's worth it."

There was a note of yearning underlying her words. Despite her ex-fiancé's betrayal, it was obvious she still longed for hearth and home with a husband who could love her fully.

He withdrew his hand from hers. He had no business

accepting her comfort when he had nothing to offer her in return. "Not all of us had such good role models."

Compassion lit her eyes. "I know. That makes it tougher—but not impossible. God gives us free will. We can choose to follow what was modeled for us, or we can choose a different path. It all comes down to choices."

"Yeah, but we also have to live with the consequences of someone else's choice." He and his dad had to suffer the results of his mother's desertion.

"True. And there are no guarantees in life."

"Right." He knew that too well. "If Dina hadn't died that night, she'd have left me anyway." As soon as the words were out, he wished he could take them back.

"Is that what you were arguing about? Had she threatened to leave you?"

Feeling sick to his soul, he nodded. "She wanted to go back to Seattle. She wanted to take Gabby. She said—" He clamped his jaw shut, trapping the words on his tongue as a bone-deep anguish threatened to split him in half.

"She said what?" Jackie prompted, her voice soft, caring.

He shook his head. He wouldn't say it. Couldn't. Because if he repeated the words Dina had flung at him, then he'd have to deal with them. And he didn't think he ever could.

Jackie touched his arm. Her small, strong and capable hand was firm and warm on his biceps. "Wyatt, whatever she said is eating away at you. The only way you'll heal is if you face it."

He swallowed hard. The need to tell Jackie became a physical ache, making his eyes burn and his chest tighten. "She said she didn't know if Gabby was my child."

Jackie let out a small gasp. "That's horrible. I'm so sorry."

Emotion tightened a noose around his throat. "I love my little girl so much."

"I know you do." There was a tender note in her voice. "Have you confirmed it?"

Confusion fogged his brain. "Confirmed what?"

"Whether Gabby is yours or not?"

Reality sharpened as her words slapped him upside the head. "It doesn't matter whose blood flows in her veins. She's my child."

"But knowing for sure would give you peace of mind."

"I'm not going to risk it. I'd rather live not knowing than face the possibility that it's true, that she's not my biological child."

"And in the meantime you'll just let it eat away at you."

His penance for not being the husband he should have been. He let his silence be his answer.

"You must have loved Dina to have married her."

He nodded slowly. "I did. She was everything I wasn't. Gregarious, creative, fun. I should have known better than to bring her here. This place stifled her. Brought out the worst in her. The worst in me."

"Not the worst. You raised Gabby together. She's a blessing from God."

His fingers flexed. A small smile tugged at the corners of his mouth. "Yes, she is."

"You'd do anything for her."

128 The Cowboy Target

"I would."

"Even if it was painful?"

He narrowed his gaze. "Yes," he said warily.

"Then find out if she's your biological child."

His jaw clenched. "I told you that is not going to happen. Gabby's paternity doesn't matter."

"But it does." She reached out to touch his shoulder. He flinched, but she didn't relent. "Knowing the truth is the only way you'll have inner peace. Knowing the truth may someday save her life."

"Plenty of people live without knowing their DNA makeup."

"And just as many suffer because of the lack of knowledge. And there's enough stories on reality shows to support my statement."

He stood abruptly. "Give it a rest. We've covered this ground, and I have no intention of doing as you suggest unless it becomes a life-threatening situation. And then only if absolutely necessary."

Watching him stalk to the bookshelf, she knew she should bite her tongue, keep back the words that were even now spilling out. "Secrets have a way of eating at a person until they crumble."

She didn't want that for Wyatt or Gabby. She knew firsthand how her ex-fiancé's secret affair had hurt when it came to light. Not only had she felt the sting of his secret, but her family—and his—had been devastated.

Just as Gabby would be if one day she learned Wyatt wasn't her biological father.

Her heart hurt for the pain Wyatt carried. Not only

inside, but she could see it also in the hunch of his shoulders and the tight lines around his mouth.

From the sound of things, his marriage had been far from blissful. Jackie wasn't naive. She knew it took two for things to go bad, but still… He blamed himself for his wife's death even though he wasn't directly responsible, and Dina's last words to him were ugly and hurtful. Words that even three years later ate away at him.

Had Dina had an affair? With whom?

That would explain the hateful things she'd said. Was Gabby Wyatt's biological child or not? That was harder to know. If Dina was so resentful of being stuck on the ranch, she might have been slinging words like arrows at Wyatt, hoping on hitting the target…his heart.

Useless anger at Dina revved through Jackie's blood.

On one hand she understood why he wouldn't pursue the truth. He was Gabby's daddy regardless of DNA. But on the other hand, not knowing was tearing him up inside.

Only the truth would bring him peace. Somehow she'd have to make him see that. Maybe then he could move on. Be content. Happy. Find love again.

An ache that wasn't physical in nature thrummed through her. She chose not to examine the cause. Doing so would only stir up longings and yearnings she had no business entertaining.

Not responding to her statement, Wyatt pulled down a book, flipped it open and plucked out a piece of paper from between the pages. He walked back to the couch, the book and paper in his hands. "I found this in my father's book."

For a moment she stared into his dark eyes, deciding whether to continue to push or to let the subject of Gabby's paternity go.

She relented. For now.

Her gaze dropped to his outstretched hand. The piece of paper he held out.

"The book from George's house?" She took the square sheet by the corner between the tips of her fingers. "What are these numbers?"

He shook his head. "I'm not sure."

She stared at numbers scrawled across the page. Could this be a clue that would lead them to George's murderer?

ELEVEN

"Maybe it's his bank account number," Wyatt said.

"Could be." She studied the digits: 41557922-104952393. "Is this George's handwriting?"

He nodded grimly. "Yes."

"It could be a life-insurance policy number or a loan number. I'll have Simone run them. She's really good at ferreting out information in the cyberworld."

"Who's Simone?" He sat back down on the couch.

"A coworker. She's the closest female friend I have. A former homicide detective out of Detroit. We bonded over our shared law-enforcement pasts."

Though Simone's past was much darker than Jackie's. Jackie had picked up on hints of this but had been unprepared when Simone had finally opened up. The painful truth had made Jackie's reasons for leaving the Atkins sheriff's department seem petty in comparison. Simone had had to make a difficult choice—to let the man who killed her childhood best friend either live or die.

In the end, her fellow officers had taken the decision out of her hands, but going through the turmoil had left a deep scar.

"I appreciate what you're doing for us," Wyatt said.

"My aunt and uncle think of you and Gabby as family."

"The feeling's mutual."

She held his gaze. A deep longing welled to the surface. She wanted to be included in those feelings of family, of belonging. Even though she had her parents and her friends at Trent, she knew there was something missing in her life. She'd never let it bother her before coming to the ranch. Now the hollow space inside of her ached like an abscessed tooth, and she was coming up empty-handed on ways to numb the pain.

She liked this man way too much.

Which didn't bode well for her peace of mind.

Yanking her gaze from his, she focused on the myriad books lining the shelves. She rose and crossed the room to read the titles on the spines. Lots of nonfiction books dealing with ranching and horses and cattle.

The fiction titles ranged from popular fiction to classics. She reached for a dog-eared copy of the complete work of Edgar Allen Poe. She could still remember reading the "The Pit and the Pendulum" in high school. She'd had to write a paper on the story. Though she'd received an A, she couldn't recall what she'd written.

"That's one of my favorites."

Wyatt's voice came from close behind her. Awareness darted down her back. The man was much too light on his feet. She replaced the volume. "Kind of dark, don't you think?"

"I went through a dark phase," he commented and reached past her to pull another thick book from the shelf.

Warmth from his big body touched her like a heat

lamp. His spicy aftershave and the fresh scent of shampoo swirled around her, making her skin tingle. She fought the yearning to turn her head and lay her cheek against the soft fabric of his shirt, to nestle into the expanse of his chest.

The sound of glass crunching from outside the window raised the fine hairs at the nape of her neck.

Reacting instantly, she reached for Wyatt with her good arm and dragged him to the ground. "Stay put," she ordered.

In a half crouch, she hurried to the couch. Before reaching for her weapon, she turned off the tableside lamp, throwing the room into darkness. She palmed her weapon and proceeded toward the window where the noise had come from. Flattening her back against the wall, she pushed aside the curtain to chance a peek out the window. A shadowy figure crept along the porch toward the front door.

"Jackie," Wyatt whispered. He moved so that he was at her elbow. "Is someone out there?"

"Shh," she hissed, wishing the man had stayed down like she'd asked. How was she supposed to protect him if he didn't cooperate? She darted toward the front door as more glass crunched beneath the stranger's feet.

Frustrated by her lame arm, Jackie debated how best to confront the trespasser and decided a confrontation wasn't the best course of action, not with Wyatt within target range.

Instead, she flipped on the porch light.

There was a muffled curse and then the pounding of footsteps as the intruder fled down the porch steps. Jackie yanked open the front door and stepped out onto the porch in time to see the man get on a motorcycle, start the engine with a loud roar and, in a spray of snow and dirt, take off down the road.

"How do you suppose he got onto the ranch without us hearing the motorbike?" Wyatt said as he halted beside her on the porch.

"Probably walked it in."

"Brilliant trick with the glass," he commented.

She followed his gaze to the smashed remains of the lightbulbs she'd sprinkled around the porch. "It worked."

"That it did."

She hustled him back inside. "I'm going to call Sheriff Landers and let him know."

"I'll check on Gabby."

Left alone in the dark living room, Jackie tried to make sense of the past two days. First there was the sloppy attempt at framing Wyatt for murder, then a professional sniper tried to take them out and now an amateur effort to break in. Something wasn't jibing. It felt as if there were two different agendas being played out here.

Still mulling over the inconsistency, she made the call to the sheriff. Not that there was much he could do because the perp got away. But he promised to keep an eye out for anyone on a motorcycle.

Settling back on the couch, Jackie's arm ached and she had the sinking feeling it was going to be a long night.

When Wyatt returned to the living room, he found Jackie on the couch looking cute, vulnerable and beat-up. Dark circles marred the delicate skin beneath her eyes. The square bandage on her forehead and the sling covering her left arm were constant reminders of their earlier ordeal. She'd had a hard knock to the head and her arm had to be hurting, yet she was toughing it out, trying to be attentive and ready to protect. The same feeling he got when he looked at the mountains on a summer night squeezed his heart.

He sat next to her on the couch and put a hand on her shoulder. "Relax. Try to rest."

She stiffened with a protest. "No, I have to stay alert."

"You won't be any good to me or Gabby exhausted," he insisted. "We'll hear if anyone disturbs the glass again. Though he'd be one dumb thug to tromp through it twice." He grinned at her.

For a moment he thought she'd bolt, but then she sat back, tucking her feet beneath her.

He hadn't asked for a bodyguard, but if he had he'd have chosen Jackie. She'd proved she was good at her job. But she was also human. And so very attractive to him.

He tugged the afghan off the back of the couch and draped it over her, then leaned back and gave in to his own exhaustion, hoping the light of day would bring a better perspective on the situation.

Jackie awoke with a start. Her heart hammered against her ribs. Wyatt's arms were wrapped around her, cocooning her in warmth. Immediately she stiffened. She couldn't remember moving into his embrace. Nor did she remember giving into sleep. She was usually much more professional. How had she allowed this to happen?

But more importantly, how did she feel about being so close to Wyatt?

She honestly didn't know.

The first rays of daylight sneaked in through the closed curtains. The house was still. Yet something had jarred her awake.

The pounding of feet running up the porch stairs, the crunch of glass and the rapid bangs of a fist against the door jerked her upright. On autopilot she reached for her weapon and sprang up. Her sore shoulder pinched with the movement, reminding her of the danger they faced.

"Wyatt! Jackie!" her uncle yelled through the closed door.

Instantly, Wyatt awoke and vaulted to his feet. Jackie made it to the door ahead of him. She yanked it open to find a haggard-looking Carl standing there. Dread exploded in her chest. Had something happened to Aunt Penny? "What's wrong?"

"It's Alexander. He's missing!"

It took a moment for her uncle's words to register. Alexander. Wyatt's prize studhorse. Missing.

She tucked her gun into her waistband.

Wyatt pushed past Jackie to stand on the porch. "Tell me what happened."

Carl ran a hand through his graying hair. "I came out this morning to feed him and the mares like always. The barn door was open, his stall empty."

"Did you check the corral?"

"Yes." Carl shook his head. "I've looked all over the ranch. I have the hands out searching the pastures now."

Without a word, Wyatt turned on his stockinged feet and disappeared back inside the house.

Jackie met her uncle's frantic gaze. "Did you hear anything last night?"

Carl rubbed his chin. "I thought I heard a motorcycle, but I didn't see anything or anyone."

Jackie nodded as new possibilities began to form in her head. "Someone tried to break into the house last night. He got away on a motorcycle." And now she wondered if the intruder last night had only been a distraction to prevent them from hearing or seeing someone taking the horse.

"This isn't good. If something happens to Alexander…" He pressed his lips together.

"What?" she asked.

"The ranch is barely afloat. Alexander's stud services are the only thing keeping Wyatt out of the red."

And losing the horse might be the thing that would force Wyatt to accept the deal offered by the Degas Corporation. Granting his mineral rights to the mining company could prove to be a lucrative endeavor. Not only for him but for his neighbors. Taking the deal would be a solution to any financial problems. But Wyatt wasn't a man motivated by money or greed. He was determined to make the ranch work on his terms. She admired that about him.

Obviously someone had different ideas about letting him conduct his business the way he wanted.

The shadow of a plane crossed her line of vision. This was the second time she'd seen a prop aircraft flying over the ranch. It flew low enough that she had no trouble making out the big numbers along the body in dark blue paint. Wyatt also had mentioned seeing a plane several times.

Was the aircraft the same one she'd seen before?

She wanted to know who owned that plane. And if they could help locate Wyatt's horse.

Wyatt returned wearing a thick leather jacket, his Stetson and cowboy boots.

"Where are you going?" Jackie asked, though she figured she knew. He wasn't the type to sit by and do nothing. He'd want to be out there searching for Alexander. Which might just be what the person targeting him wanted—Wyatt away from the protection of the main ranch.

"I'm going to find my horse," he said, confirming her suspicion.

"Not without me, you're not," Jackie stated firmly. "Uncle Carl, can you ask Aunt Penny to come over to be with Gabby?"

"Of course," Carl said. He bounded down the porch stairs and headed back to his house.

"I appreciate that you want to help—" Wyatt started to say, but he stopped when she held up a hand.

"Don't even say it. I'm coming with you to search. For your protection."

"You're injured."

She didn't need reminding. The ache in her shoulder was making itself known nicely on its own. "I can manage. Just give me a few minutes to change into some more appropriate clothing." The velour tracksuit wouldn't do for a horse-rescue mission.

His lips twisted in wry resignation. "Hurry up," he said. "I'll get the truck warmed up."

She rushed to the living room to slip her feet into her

sneakers before heading out the door and back to her aunt and uncle's to change clothes.

Gingerly she removed her arm from the sling and tossed it aside. She tested her shoulder. Though stiff and tender, she could move her arm in the socket. Careful not to jostle her shoulder overly much, she changed into jeans, a cable-knit sweater and well-worn cowboy boots her aunt lent her. She was ready to go.

She took the time to make a call to the local airstrip. The county's small airport catered to private planes.

With a few questions, she had the answer she was looking for. The plane she'd seen flying over the Monroe ranch belonged to the Degas Corporation. Her next call was to her boss, James Trent. Quickly she explained the situation.

"Sit tight and I'll call you back," he said.

Reassured that he'd know what to do, she hung up, tucked her phone next to her weapon inside the bag strapped around her waist, grabbed her jacket and headed out the door. She found Wyatt and his monster truck idling out front.

She climbed inside. "So what's your plan?"

He sat staring out the window, his hands gripping the steering wheel. "I don't have one."

Jackie's cell chirped. She dug it out and answered. James had contacted the Degas CEO. Of course he'd know the man, Jackie thought. James had contacts all over the world and in every major company. He was a man people turned to when they needed protection.

He gave her a cell number to call.

"Jackie, be careful, okay?" Trent said.

"Always." She hung up. To Wyatt she said, "I have a plan."

She called the number James had given her. A moment later a man answered. The connection wasn't good. Static crackled, making the man's voice hard to hear. "Gunderson."

"Mr. Gunderson, my name is Jackie Blain. Are you the pilot of plane 55473?"

"Yes, ma'am."

"I need your help. You've been flying pretty low over the Monroe ranch. Have you seen a black stallion roaming free?"

"As a matter of fact, yes. I saw him about an hour ago," Gunderson said. "Do you have a map of the area?"

She turned to Wyatt. "Map of the area?"

He pulled one out of the glove box and handed it to her. The map was faded and yellowed but would serve their purpose.

"I'll give you the land coordinates of where I saw the horse last," Gunderson said.

"Hold on a second." She grabbed a pen from the glove box. She held the pen over the edge of the map. "Ready."

Gunderson's voice crackled over the line as he rattled off two sets of numbers. "I'll fly back that way to see if he's still out there."

"Awesome. Thanks," she said and hung up.

She stared at the numbers she'd written. Something niggled in her brain, but she didn't have time to try to figure it out. Quickly, using the numbers, she had her finger on a spot on the map. "Here. This is where the pilot said he'd seen him last."

Wyatt took the map from her hands and studied it.

"That's in the far northeast corner of the property. We'll have to take the all-terrain vehicles."

"Let's do it," she said, hoping they could soon put an end to this whole situation once and for all.

Jackie eyed the slick-looking ATV with its big wheels, wide seat and loud motor—and smiled. She loved fast vehicles of any kind almost as much as she loved carrying a gun.

The sun was high in the sky now, its brilliant rays glistening off the packed snow and making her glad for the sun visor on the brightly colored helmet strapped on her head. Someone had produced cold-climate apparel for her. She wasn't sure whose clothes she had on. She had a sinking feeling that the thick bright green snow pants and matching jacket had once belonged to Dina Monroe.

"Sure you're up for this?" Wyatt asked for the hundredth time.

She cut him a glance. He'd changed into snow gear much like what she now wore, only his clothes were bright orange. "Yes. I told you. I'm fine."

Skepticism shone in his eyes. "You sure you know how to drive one of these?"

"What makes you think I wouldn't?"

He shrugged. "Not much use for an ATV in Boston."

"Ah, but you forget I was raised in Iowa. Besides, my daddy and grandpa would take me to Montana with them during hunting season. We packed our gear on ATVs."

To prove the point, she threw her leg over the engine block and plunked down on the black leather seat. She placed her hands on the handlebars and put her right

foot on the back brake pedal. She reached forward between the bars to turn the engine key. An orange light
on the panel glowed. With her left hand, she squeezed
the choke and used her thumb to push the start button.
The engine came to life with a deep rumble. Using her
right hand, she twisted the handle and the ATV moved
forward. She adjusted the choke and did a lap around
the driveway. When she halted where she'd started, she
looked expectantly at Wyatt.

He nodded. "All right. Scoot back."

The plan was for them to ride double until they found
Alexander, then Wyatt would ride the horse back while
she drove the ATV. The rig was laden with a bridle and
reins, a side bag filled with water, food prepared by
Aunt Penny and two sleeping bags. Jackie sure hoped
the bags were a just-in-case type of deal.

She did not want to spend the night out in the nether
regions of the Monroe property. Sleeping on the hard
ground didn't appeal to her. She'd never been one for
camping without a few luxuries—like an air mattress,
for starters.

Wyatt settled himself in front of her. The scent of his
aftershave hung on the cold air. Fighting to keep from
nuzzling closer to get a better whiff, she wrapped her
arms around his waist. The solid feel of him sent a thrill
chasing up her spine.

Feeling awkward and guilty for the attraction zinging
through her blood, she glanced over her shoulder to see
Spencer and Gabby standing with Penny on the porch.
Jackie waved. Gabby blew kisses. Jackie's heart melted.
She blew a kiss back to the little princess.

They moved along at a nice clip away from the ranch.

She didn't want to hang on to him so tightly, but she had no choice. Every point of contact burned right through the thick material of her snowsuit.

For the next several hours, they wound their way across pasturelands, startling cattle and birds. They stopped several times to open and close gates as they moved from one cordoned-off section into another.

Jackie had known the Monroe property was big, but the reality of just how much land the man owned made her wonder why he didn't sell some if he was having money troubles. But a man's pride was a prickly monster, she supposed.

They stopped to eat and stretch near the base of a burr oak in what Wyatt referred to as the calving pasture. The rough bark with its many furrows made for a good break from the wind that had kicked up. Overhead clouds rolled in from the east over the mountain, dimming the winter sun.

Jackie opened the side bag on the ATV and pulled out a sack with two hard bread rolls stuffed with cold cuts, cheese and dill pickles. Just the way she liked her sandwiches. Wyatt, however, had a sandwich piled high with turkey and lettuce between slices of multigrain bread.

"Uncle Carl mentioned that you're having some money problems," she said between bites.

Wyatt's eyebrows rose, then lowered as he faced away from her. "Your uncle should keep my business private."

"He didn't mean any harm. He's worried about Alexander. About what it would mean to the ranch if something happens to the horse."

"The stallion does generate a healthy income," he said

and took a swig from his water bottle. "But the ranch is doing fine. I have investments that keep us afloat."

"Investments?"

"Stocks, mostly. But I have shares in a few real-estate properties around the state."

"Then why does Uncle Carl believe the ranch isn't fiscally sound?"

"My private investments aren't part of the ranch's assets. I move money over when needed."

She'd already learned the man was more than he seemed. Poe and Dickens. Cattle and studhorses. The stock market and real estate. Shrewd businessman and cowboy. A man of depth. A man worth loving.

She coughed as a bite of her sandwich went down wrong. Wyatt looked at her questioningly, and she waved him off. She wasn't choking. Nor was she falling in love.

She cared, sure. But that was as far as she could allow herself to go. Getting emotionally involved put her at risk of heartbreak. Once in a lifetime was enough. Never again. "We better get moving," she said crisply and started packing up their supplies.

In the distance, the rev of an engine whining as it accelerated sent a shiver of alarm down her spine.

TWELVE

"A snowmobile," she stated grimly. "Hurry."

She jammed the last of her lunch into the pack and jumped on the ATV behind Wyatt. He started the motor. The sound of the approaching snowmobile grew louder, but the machine wasn't visible yet.

In a spray of snow, Wyatt took off, opening the throttle all the way, pushing the machine to its limits. Air whipped against her face as the ATV flew over the rough terrain. The slight discomfort in her shoulder barely registered. She glanced back just as the snowmobile came into view over a ridge. The driver wore all white. It had to be the same man who'd shot at them yesterday. A flash of fear ratcheted up the knot of tension forming in her gut. The type of high-powered rifle the shooter had was a deadly threat. One she wasn't sure how to stop.

Heart pounding beneath her ribs, she debated their options. They couldn't outrun the snowmobile. Best to face the oncoming threat. Fisting the back of Wyatt's jacket in her left hand to keep from flying off, she reached inside her coat for her gun. Twisting at the waist so that she faced the snowmobile, she took aim, waiting for their pursuer to come within range.

She fired one shot. Missed. Hard to hit a moving target. Especially one going more than fifty miles an hour. But even still, the man on the snowmobile veered to the right and looped back the way he'd come, disappearing over the ridge in the landscape.

Wyatt slowed the ATV to a stop. "He's gone."

Realizing she was frozen with her weapon aimed at nothing, she gave herself a shake and lowered her gun. Inhaling deeply, she let the adrenaline rush out. She sagged forward to lean her head on his shoulder, grateful for his solid, broad back. She was thankful the Lord had spared them. But how long until their assailant came back? Next time he'd have the tactical rifle he'd used to blow out the tire on her SUV. If anything happened to Wyatt, she'd never forgive herself.

Protecting Wyatt just might cost her her life...and her heart.

"Jackie?"

The concern in Wyatt's voice brought her upright. "We need to hurry and find your horse."

With a grim nod, he faced forward and hit the gas. But Jackie couldn't shake the feeling of danger breathing down her neck.

As they reached the edge of the property line where the Monroe ranch met the Dunns' spread, Wyatt slowed the machine beneath him; his gaze searched the landscape in the fading light. Evening was fast approaching, and soon it would be too dark to search for the horse.

A black lump on the ground near the creek bed on this side of the fence made Wyatt's heart thump and his stomach drop with dread. Alexander.

He gestured to Jackie and sped up. As they approached the horse, the animal lifted his head and whinnied. His dark eyes showed white with fear and panic.

Cutting the engine, Wyatt jumped from the ATV, grabbed the halter and lead rope he'd brought, and ran to Alexander's side. "It's okay, boy. I'm here now."

The horse immediately stopped tossing his head and settled. Alexander tried to stand, but his legs collapsed beneath him. Wyatt quickly realized the problem. The horse's front right leg was trapped knee-deep in the earth.

Jackie slid to the ground next to Wyatt. She'd removed her helmet. Her wild blond curls spilled over her shoulders. "He's hurt?"

"Yeah, he's stepped into some kind of crevice." Keeping a hand on Alexander's shoulder, Wyatt inspected the opening. It was a perfectly round hole. An icy foreboding gripped the back of his neck. "This isn't natural. Someone made this."

Leaning close so she could see, Jackie asked, "Can you free him?"

"I think so. In one of the packs is a small trowel."

"I'll get it."

Wyatt yanked his helmet off and tossed it aside. He worked to put the halter over the horse's head. He let the lead rope dangle to the ground as he concentrated on keeping Alexander calm by stroking his coat and talking gently to him.

Jackie returned with a stainless-steel folding trowel. "Here you go."

Using the sharp tip, he worked to widen the hole. Sweat broke out on his back, but he didn't take the time to remove the heavy parka. The earth slowly loosened around Alexander's leg. He sat back. "Okay. We're going to have to get him up so we can release his forelock and hoof."

"What do you want me to do?"

"I'm going to help him stand. Once he's upright, you grasp him by the knee." He showed her where. "Then tug for all you're worth."

He sure hoped Jackie would be strong enough. Especially with her injured shoulder.

"Come on, boy. Time to stand," Wyatt coaxed. He positioned himself near the horse's girth; he slid his hand beneath Alexander's belly and flexed his arms. The horse whinnied and twitched. "Up, boy. You can do it."

Alexander struggled to get his hind feet under him. Wyatt lifted, his muscles straining. Jackie grasped Alexander by the knee. She let out a groan as the right hoof popped out of the ground. She let go and tumbled onto her backside. Alexander broke from Wyatt's arms and tried to run, but as soon as he put weight on the right hoof, the leg buckled and he went down. Jackie gave a small cry. Wyatt flinched and rushed to the horse as he struggled to regain his footing.

Once upright, Alexander pulled his bad leg up, balancing on the tip of the hoof. Blood dripped from a gash on the front of his cannon bone. Holding on to the lead rope, Wyatt carefully inspected the bones of the right leg. He didn't detect a break. But he wouldn't breathe a sigh of relief until a vet took a look. He pulled out his cell phone. No signal. Frustration pounded against his temple.

"I can't get a signal out here," Wyatt stated grimly.

"There's no way he can walk all the way back." He'd end up lame, and Wyatt would have to put him down. "If only I'd thought to bring a splint."

"You couldn't have anticipated he'd be hurt, Wyatt."

"I should have planned for the possibility, though. I should have—" He cut himself off, his frustration as imposing as the mountains behind them. He had to deal with this.

"And I should have predicted we'd be chased on your land by some guy on a snowmobile," Jackie stated.

"There was no reason to believe—" Her arched eyebrow stopped him.

"Yeah, two can play the self-flagellation game." She shook her head. "But it doesn't accomplish anything. We need to move forward. Make a plan."

Leave it to Jackie to put him in his place. He liked that about her. She wasn't afraid to speak her mind.

"One of us will have to make the ride back to the ranch alone while the other stays with Alexander," he said.

She eyed the horse with concern and nodded. "Then you better head to the ranch and bring help."

He glanced at the setting sun hanging low over the horizon. He hated the thought of leaving Jackie out here with the injured horse, but he doubted she'd be able to find her way back to the ranch in the dark. "I'll head back far enough to get a signal. I'll have Carl contact the vet and come out here with a trailer. They can reach us if they drive over the Dunns' property."

"Boyd Dunn?"

"Yeah." Wyatt grimaced. "Boyd's dad, Frank, owns the land on the other side of the fence. I'm not sure how cooperative the Dunn family will be, though. There's no love lost between our families."

"Why's that?"

"One of the biggest sources of conflict is the creek." He gestured toward the slow-moving body of water a few paces away. "The Dunns want access to the water, but their property ends two feet shy of the creek's edge. I've offered to sell them the land, but Frank Dunn wants it for free."

"Ah, I can see how that would create tension."

He could only hope Frank Dunn would give them some grace and allow Carl and the vet to traverse his property to get here. Wyatt had no problem with breaking down part of the fence to get Alexander out. However, he'd no doubt have to fix the fence with improvements.

"Why don't I take the ATV and make the call?" Jackie said, her gaze troubled. "There's still the guy on the snowmobile to think about."

"True. But it'll be dark soon. If snowmobile guy comes after me, I can run. I know this land by heart. You don't." He cupped her cheek in his palm, which felt smooth and soft against his calloused skin. "Don't worry. I'll come back in one piece."

She blinked, then turned her head slightly to press her lips against his palm. His heart tripped over itself. Emotions rose to clog his throat. Now was not the time to analyze what he felt.

"Be careful," she whispered.

"I will."

He backed away, from her and from the feelings rising from the depths of his heart. Though a tangible threat lurked somewhere in the dark, a different kind of danger hovered close—the danger of losing his heart to Jackie. And that was something he couldn't allow to happen. Not if he wanted to avoid the burn of heartache again. An inevitable ending. Soon she'd leave, go back to her life in Boston—and he'd be left here hurting.

Jackie watched Wyatt ride away on the ATV. A strange sense of loneliness threatened to overwhelm her. She crossed her arms over her chest, then shook off the feeling. He would be back, she reasoned. It wasn't as if she'd never see him again.

Though if snowmobile guy had his way...

The thought of Wyatt hurt caused a knot of fear in her midsection. "Lord, please watch over Wyatt. Keep him safe."

She had to trust that God would protect Wyatt. There was no other choice. His safety at the moment was out of her control. But she hated feeling so useless and anxious. Inhaling deeply, she strove to remain calm and find peace in trusting Wyatt to God's care.

Needing something to do, she turned her attention to Alexander. She could at least care for the horse. Alexander meant so much to Wyatt. She could show the horse the care and affection she was afraid to show his owner.

With lead rope in hand, she led him slowly to the creek's edge. The horse limped along without a noise of complaint.

"Thirsty, boy?"

He dipped his head and slurped at the water.

Placing her hand on his right shoulder, she ran her hand down his bad leg until she reached his knee. Alexander picked up his foot and offered his upturned hoof to her. Fearing she'd hurt him, she released his leg.

The blood had dried on the wound. She wished she had a cloth or something to wash the blood away. She settled for splashing water on the gash and washing away the blood to reveal the open wound. Wishing for something to wrap around the gash, she thought about taking off her undershirt, but the temperature had dropped significantly, and a shiver worked its way over her body. Not far away she'd seen an outcropping of boulders. The rocks would provide some shelter from the wind.

"Come on, boy." Slowly, they picked their way toward the dark mass of rocks.

Alexander's ears perked up as a noise filled the air. Headlights cut through the darkness. The sound of tires crunching over the ground made Jackie's heart pound. It was too soon for Uncle Carl to arrive. Where was Wyatt?

Her gaze searched the inky landscape where he'd ridden off. But there was no sign of him returning. Was he hurt? Dying?

She peeked around the side of the boulder. A pickup truck came to a stop on the other side of the fence not far from where Alexander had been injured. Three men emerged from the truck. It was too dark to see their faces, but she could make out the baseball cap of one and the cowboy hat of another. The third man didn't have any head covering, but he wore a long coat that flapped behind him as he walked toward the fence.

"This is the spot?"

Jackie wasn't positive, but she was pretty sure the man speaking was Pendleton, the Degas Corporation's representative.

Alexander nudged her shoulder. She stroked his nose but kept her attention on the men.

"Yep. The guys you sent over to take samples bored several holes here and on the other side of the fence. They confirmed it," one of the other men said. His voice sounded vaguely familiar. His words stirred anger on Wyatt's behalf. They were surveying on his land without his consent. And Alexander had stepped into one of their holes.

"You'll never get Monroe's permission to drill on his side of the creek," the third man said. He stood in the military-at-ease pose—hands resting low at his back, his spine straight, his feet braced slightly apart. She'd seen her colleague Kyle Martin stand similarly. Kyle had been a SEAL before joining Trent Associates. Deeply ingrained habits were hard to break. "Especially when he learns what's down there."

"We'll see," Pendleton said. "The man has to have a price. We just have to figure out what it is. The uranium's worth billions."

Shock reverberated through her. Uranium? She shuddered at the thought of the radioactive heavy metal used for nuclear energy. No way would Wyatt ever let the land be destroyed to mine uranium. Not to mention the health risks unearthing that stuff would unleash.

Her gaze went to the creek. Was the water tainted?

Was this the secret George had been murdered for? Her mind flashed back to the note she'd found in his house.

KEEP YOUR MOUTH SHUT OR ELSE.

Had he found out about the surveying? The uranium?

"He won't bend," the third man said with a hard edge

to his voice. "I know him. They don't get any more stubborn than Wyatt Monroe."

"That stubbornness might end up being his downfall," Pendleton stated.

The ominous words lingered in the air. She shuddered.

The men climbed back into the truck and drove away.

She leaned back against the rock face. That sounded distinctly like a threat to Wyatt's well-being. Was Pendleton the one behind everything that had happened? Was he the sniper? The arsonist? The one who let Alexander out?

No. Pendleton struck her as the type who hired others to do his dirty work. But would he really put himself and the corporation he worked for at risk by being part of something illegal? Or would the Degas Corporation sanction such actions?

She checked her watch. To keep herself warm, she jogged in place. Soon the sound of the ATV returning filled her ears. When Wyatt arrived, relief to see him alive and well, mixed with something closer to happiness, rushed through her. Not caring that she was acting like a woman whose man had just returned to her from a long trip, she rushed to his side and slipped her arms around his waist.

"What took you so long?" she asked, wincing slightly at the needy thread woven through her tone. She wasn't needy. What was that about?

His arms encircled her in warmth and strength, making her feel safe. Crazy—because it was her job to protect him. But this heady rush of comfort had nothing to do with the physical threat looming ever closer and everything to do with the crumbling of her defenses.

"Sorry. I had a hard time finding a signal," Wyatt said. "Carl and the vet should be here soon."

Snuggling into his embrace, she savored the moment before she stepped back and told him about Pendleton and what she'd overheard.

"Uranium? Unbelievable." Anger punctuated each word. "No way. No way will I let that happen."

"I think one of the men who was with Pendleton was Boyd. I didn't recognize the other man's voice and I couldn't see what he looked like, other than that he wore a hat like the one you wear and had the bearing of a military man."

"Most likely Darrin Dunn, Boyd's older brother. He joined the marines right out of high school. Came back about five years ago. But last I heard he was living over in Laramie running some sort of business."

"Interesting." A marine. Definitely someone who would know how to handle a high-powered rifle. Might even have one he'd bought off the black market during a tour somewhere and smuggled home.

"Figures the Dunns would be in on this." Wyatt blew out a breath, no doubt trying to calm his ire. "They've wanted to buy the Monroe ranch since I was a kid. Frank Dunn and my dad had been friends at one time, but then when my dad started his downward spiral, Frank tried to pressure him into selling. Dad wouldn't. Neither would I when Frank approached me."

Though she couldn't see his features clearly, she knew every plane and angle of his face by heart. "When we get back we need to talk to Sheriff Landers."

"Sounds like a plan."

A chill snaked through her. She rubbed her arms and stomped her feet. She sure wished her uncle would arrive.

"You're cold," Wyatt stated and drew her back into his embrace.

She laid her head on his chest, grateful for his warmth. He smoothed a hand down her back. She knew staying in his embrace wasn't smart—doing so wouldn't lead her anywhere she wanted to go—but under the cloak of darkness, in the isolation of the land, she didn't care. For now, she was right where she wanted to be—clinging to Wyatt Monroe.

Tomorrow in the light of day she'd deal with the pain of knowing this wouldn't last. Couldn't last. She wasn't willing to put her heart and her life into someone else's hands. She could never give anyone that much power again.

"Jackie? What are we doing?"

The husky timbre of his voice sent a shiver of responsiveness through her nerve endings, setting her heart on fire. She didn't answer because she didn't know. She only knew what she was feeling at the moment, and for now that was all that mattered. She tilted her head up so she could look at him. She slid her arms around his shoulders until her hands found the sides of his face. The coarse hairs of his late-evening beard prickled her palms as she drew his head toward her.

"Jackie."

The way he said her name, the warning, the yearning and heat in the word, prompted her to close the gap between them. She leaned forward, raising her chin. Her lips molded over his. He remained motionless.

A panicked flutter of embarrassment threatened to engulf her, then his lips moved, gentle and rough all at once. Delight blossomed inside her, making the world spin. His arms tightened, drawing her closer until she felt the wild thump of his heart beating in time with hers, and she knew she wasn't alone in the strong grip of attraction.

As she gave herself over to the sensations erupting inside of her, the world lit up, as if they were generating enough electricity between them to glow as bright as a torchlight.

Wyatt eased his lips away and rested his forehead against hers. "We've got company."

Headlights bathed them in spotlight. Mortified to be caught kissing like a pair of teenagers in the backseat of a car, she groaned and squeezed her eyes tight. "They saw us, huh?"

"Yeah, I'd say so."

Amusement danced in his tone. This was funny to him? She swatted at him and stepped back, putting distance between them. Immediately she regretted the space and wanted to regain each step back into his arms.

She whirled around to face the three vehicles stopping on the other side of the fence. Putting up a hand to shield her eyes from the headlights, she saw that one of the trucks had a horse trailer hitched to the back.

These people knew Wyatt well. They had seen them kissing. Her cheeks heated even more. She'd acted unprofessionally and been caught. Her uncle had seen the kiss. Would he disapprove? She didn't want to do anything to mess up her life or Wyatt's. There couldn't be any more kissing.

No how matter much her lips tingled and her heart cried for another.

THIRTEEN

Doors opened and slammed shut. Uncle Carl hurried to the fence, along with a woman with a long dark braid sticking out of a dark beanie cap. Carl halted by the fence while the woman ducked between the slats and hurried to Alexander.

"That's Janis, the vet," Wyatt explained to Jackie.

"I'll see if she needs help," Jackie said and peeled away from him.

Running a hand through his hair, he expelled a quick breath. He felt jumbled up inside. He'd kissed Jackie. Or rather, he'd responded to her kiss.

He had trouble comprehending that she'd made the first move. Or had he, by taking her into his arms?

Holding her had felt so natural, just as it had the night before. He could get used to having Jackie around, in his arms, kissing him.

Better not let himself go any further with those kinds of thoughts. Better to remember the reality of his life. He wasn't husband material. He had nothing to offer a woman like Jackie. Best to focus on the issues he could do something about.

Wyatt's gaze went to the elderly gentleman approach-

ing the fence. His shockingly white hair glowed in the
headlights. He seemed to have a more pronounced stoop
to his shoulders beneath the heavy corduroy jacket than
he'd had the last time Wyatt had seen him. But the fierce
scowl on his weathered face was familiar and churned
renewed anger in Wyatt's belly.

"Frank."

"Monroe. Heard you got yourself into some trouble
out here," Frank Dunn stated in a gruff growl. He had
a claw-ended hammer in one hand, while he draped the
other arm over the fence post.

"More like trouble thrust upon me," Wyatt muttered.
He waded across the shallow water to stand opposite the
older man, with the fence slats separating them.

"Things aren't that bad if your idea of trouble in-
volves kissing pretty women in the snow."

Ignoring the comment and the heat creeping up his
neck, Wyatt said, "I don't appreciate people coming
on my land and drilling holes without my permission."

Frank frowned. "I don't know what you're jabbering
about. And I don't like your tone."

"You tell your sons to stay off my property," Wyatt
shot back, not believing for a second that the old man
didn't know what his boys were up to.

"Seems to me you're in no position to be making de-
mands, seeing as how I'm allowing your foreman and
the vet here to drive across my land to come to your rescue," Frank countered with an arched eyebrow.

Wyatt reined in his anger. He needed Frank's cooperation to get Alexander back to the ranch. "I appreciate your allowing Carl and Janis access."

"Yeah, well. Let's get this done. It's late and my old

bones don't like the cold." He used the claw to pry out the nails holding the slats to the fence post.

Right now the issue of the illegal surveying could wait, but first thing tomorrow Wyatt was going to have a chat with the sheriff—and then Pendleton. And, God willing, put an end to the threat hanging over his life.

By the time they had transported Alexander back to Wyatt's ranch and the vet had left, dawn had broken with a vibrant array of reds and hues of gold against a crystal-blue sky. Thankfully the vet had determined the horse would recover. The gash wasn't deep and the bones in his leg weren't broken, only bruised, but even to Jackie's untrained eye, he was obviously sore.

Still, relief wasn't giving Jackie a second wind. She could hardly keep her eyes open. She needed coffee in a bad way. All the way back, she'd watched for a tail, for any sign of a snowmobile-riding sniper, but thankfully none had dared appear. She was keeping an alert eye out to prevent herself from dwelling too much on the kiss she and Wyatt had shared. Later, when she was alone, she'd relive the moment and savor the memory. Because that was all she'd ever have. Once this threat against Wyatt was resolved, she'd return to her life and he to his. End of story.

"Come on," Wyatt said, slipping an arm around her waist and propelling her out of the barn toward her aunt and uncle's place. "You need sleep."

As good as it felt to have him near her, she eased away. Getting used to touches and caresses wasn't a smart idea. "Can't. Need to talk to the sheriff first."

Wyatt stopped to face her. "We will. But it's not even

6:00 a.m. yet. We'll go see him later, when we're rested and coherent."

"Speak for yourself, bucko. I'm coherent. I just need coffee."

"Coffee will give you a jolt, but it won't last. Then you'll crash and be worse off."

His concern for her well-being touched her. What he said was true, but she didn't want to let him out of her sight. Not with someone out there gunning for him. "I have to stay with you. You're not safe without me."

He arched a dark eyebrow. "I think I can chance it for a few hours. Besides, it's daylight and there are a dozen hands working around here, plus Carl. If anyone who doesn't belong comes near the ranch, someone will see them. I've explained the situation to the hands. They'll keep an eye out for anything suspicious."

Used to working with a team, she appreciated that there were others on the ranch who had a vested interest in protecting Wyatt. Still, it was her job to guard him. "I can rest on your couch while you sleep," she insisted on a yawn.

One corner of his mouth tipped upward at the corner. "Not happening. I won't sleep knowing you're so close. Not when all I want to do is kiss you again."

His words sent a little thrill sliding over her skin. Memories of their kiss last night rushed to the forefront of her mind, and a heated blush crept up her neck while she yearned for a repeat performance. The look in his eyes made her tummy flutter like a million butterflies taking flight.

Better to step back from the edge of insanity than to give in to the longing coursing through her veins.

For now she'd have to trust God and the ranch hands to stand guard while she and Wyatt both took some short downtime. She needed time to shower and change, at least. A catnap would be wonderful, too. "I'll go to Aunt Penny's."

He laughed. "You do that."

"Only for a few hours," she amended. "Then we head to town to talk to the sheriff. Agreed?"

"Agreed."

Yet neither moved. Emotions swirled through Jackie, each flittering through so quickly that she was struggling to grasp one long enough to examine. Attraction, longing, caring and something deeper, something that made her head pound and her heart squeeze tight. Must be the fatigue, she decided. Time to retreat, regroup and recharge before she did something totally stupid—like tell Wyatt she was rapidly on her way to falling for him. In a big way. She turned on her heel and made a break for the front door.

Wyatt watched Jackie hurry away toward her aunt and uncle's house as though he'd lit a fire under her feet. Guilt washed over him. He rubbed a hand over his face. What was he doing? He'd told himself he wouldn't go down this road. Wouldn't allow his heart to get involved again. Kissing her last night had been a mistake because it made the attraction he'd been fighting rage out of control. In the light of day, he realized attraction wasn't the only thing he was feeling. He more than liked Jackie. She was everything he could ever want or hope for in a woman. Smart, capable, loyal and compassionate. Plus, Gabby adored her. He adored her.

He spun away and looked around the ranch that was his heart and soul, second only to Gabby. The March snow was melting as the weather grew warmer today, making the droplets of water dripping from the roofline of the house appear like diamonds as they fell to the porch. The land stretched out in all directions with no visible signs of human life, only horses and cattle for miles. Closer in, men worked to clear away the debris from the burned-out shed. Soon a new feed shed would be built, and life would resume its normal rhythm.

This wasn't the life for a woman like Jackie. She thrived on action, adventure and challenge. She carried a handgun as though it was an extension of herself. She'd never be content here.

Just as Dina hadn't been.

A knot of tension tightened in his chest. Wyatt couldn't go through that kind of turmoil again. He wouldn't put Gabby through losing another mother.

Best to put the brakes on whatever was happening between them now before either of them got hurt. He may not have initiated the kiss last night, but he'd brought it up today. Bad idea. He couldn't do that again, no matter how tempting her kisses were.

With that thought planted firmly in place, he headed to the house to see his daughter, even as his heart broke just a little bit.

"Jackie! Jackie, wake up!"

Uncle Carl's voice penetrated through the deep sleep Jackie had succumbed to the second her head hit the pillow. Flipping from her side to her back, she pried her eyes open and blinked at the sudden light. It was still daytime but looked to be late afternoon by the way the sun hung low in the sky outside her window. Her catnap had gone on too long. Her uncle stood at the foot of the bed, concern etched on his craggy face.

Immediately she came fully awake. She sat up, her heart pounding. "What's wrong?"

"Wyatt left."

"Left?" She swung her feet off the edge of the bed and stood. For a moment, the world tilted as blood rushed to her head. She braced her feet apart and waited for the dizziness to pass. As soon as it did, she faced her uncle. "What happened?"

"He came over with Gabby a few minutes ago and said he had to take care of something. I told him he should wait for you, but he wouldn't. I'm worried."

She grabbed her cell phone off the bedside table. "What's his number?"

As he rattled off the number, she dialed. The call went to Wyatt's voice mail. "Wyatt, it's Jackie. Call me ASAP."

A groan of frustration broke from her as she strapped on an ankle holster with her backup piece secured in the soft leather sleeve. Stubborn, bullheaded, reckless. She yanked her pant leg down over the holster and stuffed her feet into her boots. Was he trying to get himself killed? Did he like stepping into danger? Had he given any thought to Gabby?

She had to find him. She had to keep him safe. Leaving him had been a mistake. But she couldn't have anticipated he'd take off without her.

After attaching her hip holster at her waist, she contemplated her next move. First place to start was at the house. She hurried across the drive and entered the Monroe home. For a moment she stood stock-still in the entryway as she considered the best place to look for some clue as to where he'd gone. She went to his office and rounded the desk to sit in his leather chair. She studied the desk.

Neat and tidy, yet showing signs of Wyatt.

A half-filled coffee mug, a small bowl of almonds within reach. His computer was off. She contemplated firing it up, but she didn't know his passwords and would only waste time trying to figure them out. A notepad and pen lay on the desk.

She ran her fingers over the pad. She could feel the indentation where the pen had dug into the paper. She opened the desk drawer and found a pencil. Using the edge of the pointed tip, she lightly shaded over the indentations.

A set of numbers appeared in the etching. From the prefix, she guessed the number belonged to a local phone. She looked around and realized there was no landline in the office. She dug out her cell phone and dialed the number.

After a few rings a female voice answered. "Whiskey Saloon."

Jackie frowned. "Saloon?"

"Yeah. What can I do for you?"

"Uh, who is this?"

"Pearl. Who's this?"

"I'm looking for Wyatt Monroe."

"He's not here."

Jackie thanked the woman and hung up. Why would Wyatt write down the bar's phone number? Maybe the number had been on the pad for a long time and had nothing to do with what was going on now.

But it gave her an idea. She quickly dialed Trent Associates. When her coworker Simone answered, Jackie greeted her warmly, then asked, "Hey, could you contact Anthony Carlucci and ask him to run a cell number for me? I want the last incoming and last outgoing numbers."

Carlucci was their contact in the Department of Justice. As a former Secret Service agent and lawyer, he'd joined Trent Associates for a short time and taken on one assignment, protecting the widow and son of a U.S. senator from a ruthless killer. By the time the threat was neutralized, Anthony had fallen in love with the widow, prompting him to join the DOJ and move permanently to Washington to be with the woman and child.

"Is this an emergency?" Simone asked, reminding Jackie that reaching out to Carlucci was reserved for emergencies only. Trent didn't want to abuse the connection.

Jackie winced. She wasn't sure if this situation constituted an emergency or not. But she wasn't taking any chances. Not with a murderer loose. "Enough of one."

"Then give me the number."

Jackie did.

"I'll call you back in a few," Simone promised.

Secure in knowing Simone was a woman of her word, Jackie decided there wasn't anything more to find in the office. She headed back to the living room. Lying on the coffee table was the book Wyatt had taken from George's house.

Next to it was the slip of paper with the odd numbers

that Wyatt had found lodged inside the book. She'd forgotten about it in the chaos of someone trying to break in and then Alexander going missing. She stared at the numbers. They seemed familiar. She called Simone back.

"Impatient much?" Simone said with a laugh when Jackie identified herself.

"You know it," Jackie replied. "Actually, I have another request. Wyatt found something that might be a clue as to who killed his ranch hand. It's a set of numbers. Too many for a phone. I'm thinking maybe a bank account."

"Give 'em to me and I'll see what I can come up with."

Jackie read off the long set of digits. If anyone could figure out the puzzling numbers, it was Simone. She was gifted that way.

"Hmm. Could be an account number of some sort. But you know what I think— Hold on a second. I want to check something."

Simone returned to the line a few seconds later. "They're coordinates. Longitude and latitude."

Of course. They were the same ones the pilot had given her, the numbers that had pointed to the place where Alexander stepped into a borehole. The place where the Degas Corporation had been surveying on Wyatt's land.

Not exactly proof that the Degas representative was George's murderer, but...

"Anthony got back to me with those numbers on the cell you wanted," Simone said, breaking through her thoughts.

"Can you text them to my cell?"

"Sure thing," Simone said. "Jackie, be careful, okay?"

"Always." She hung up, and almost immediately the text came through. She glanced at the numbers and decided to start with the incoming call.

A few seconds later a man answered. "Hello?"

"Hello. You called Wyatt Monroe today. Can you tell me why?"

"Who are you?"

Fair enough question. "I'm Jackie Blain. I'm staying at the Monroe ranch. I need to find Wyatt. It's important. Can you help me?"

"I told Wyatt there was something fishy going on along our mutual property line."

Drilling? "Did you call the sheriff, Mr...?" She was pretty sure this wasn't a Dunn but one of Wyatt's other neighbors.

"No. Wyatt said he'd take care of it."

Great. She hurried back to the office. "Can you tell me where exactly?" Picking up the pen, she added, "I'll need directions from the Monroe ranch."

She wrote as the man gave her instructions. After hanging up, she called the sheriff and told him what was happening. He promised to meet her there. Because her rented SUV was now in the body shop after taking a header into a ditch, she was without wheels. Thinking about the crash reminded her of her shoulder. Though a bit stiff and sore when tested to its limit, it was usable.

She rushed back to her uncle. "I need to borrow your truck."

"Did you find out where Wyatt went?" Carl asked, handing her the keys.

"I did." She told him what the neighbor had said. "Guy didn't give me his name."

"Hmm. If it's the neighbor to the north, it would have to be Josh Freeman." Carl walked her to the truck. "Call when you find Wyatt, okay?"

"I will." She settled behind the wheel. As she started the engine, she sent up a prayer. "Lord, I'm trusting you've got Wyatt's back until I can get there. I trust you'll have my back, too."

She followed the directions, taking the main road and winding around the ranch to the north. She turned down a dirt road running along the fence, then came to a locked gate and halted. The land was flat for as far as the eye could see. Cattle huddled in small groups, and a few trees sprung out of the ground here and there. Where was Wyatt?

Wishing she had binoculars, she tapped her fingers on the steering wheel, contemplating her next move. Why did she think the guy on the phone had told her the truth? Had she even been talking to Josh Freeman?

Feeling like she'd made a rookie blunder, she called Simone back. "Hey again."

"You okay?" Concern laced Simone's tone. "Did you find your guy?"

"No." Her gut churned with anxiety. "Remember that incoming number you gave me for that cell? Can you tell me who it belongs to?"

"Let me check the info Anthony sent over. Hold on a second."

Tension tightened the muscles in her shoulders as she waited for Simone to return to the line.

When she did, she said, "It's a burner phone."

Dread squeezed her in a fierce grip. She'd been had. Dumb mistake. "What about the outgoing call?"

"It's an unlisted number. Give me a second. There are all kinds of internet sites that I can search and find what we need. You know there is no such thing as privacy anymore."

The sound of computer keys clicking in rapid tempo matched the beat of Jackie's heart. The seconds were ticking by, and the longer Wyatt was out there alone, the more chance he was in danger.

Or he could be out shopping for supplies, for all she knew. She really hated feeling so helpless and so emotionally tied to his well-being. And that was exactly how she felt. Tied to him by some invisible cord she hadn't seen coming or expected.

She was rapidly falling for the handsome cowboy.

There. She acknowledged what her heart was feeling. Didn't mean she was going to do anything about it. Except save his hide—if she could find him. Then she'd bail out of town as fast as she could before she dug herself any deeper into an emotional abyss.

"Got it," Simone said. "Number belongs to Frank Dunn. Name ring any bells?"

Her stomach dropped. She should have known. The disgruntled neighbor. "Yes. It sure does."

FOURTEEN

"What's this about, Frank?" Wyatt focused his gaze on the older man standing before him in the Dunn barn. The smells of horses and hay permeated the air.

When Boyd Dunn had called, telling Wyatt that Boyd's daddy wanted to talk to him, Wyatt had called the elder Dunn, who said he'd only talk in person and asked if Wyatt could come out to the ranch.

After leaving Gabby in Penny and Carl's care, Wyatt had driven to the Dunns' ranch. Carl had tried to talk him into waiting for Jackie. He'd debated doing so but decided he'd rather she were there with Gabby than with him.

Gabby's safety was more important than his own.

It wasn't that he didn't trust Carl and Penny to protect his child, but having a professional bodyguard watching over his daughter gave him peace of mind. Besides, he was only going to the Dunns' to talk to Frank.

"We want you to reconsider your position on mining your land," Frank stated.

Men and a few women from the neighboring ranches surrounded him. Slowly, he turned to stare each of the six people in the eye. "You all think you can intimidate me into signing over my mineral rights? Is that it?"

"We just want you to see reason," Josh Freeman said. "Some of us are barely making ends meet. The money from the minerals would make a huge difference in our lives."

"I've got the bank breathing down my neck," another man, Ed Wright, commented. "We could sure use the money that company is offering us. But they won't deal unless you cooperate."

Wyatt understood their plight. He really did. But how did a financial crisis on their part constitute the need for him to bend his principles? "Do you even know what mineral they want to take from the ground?"

"It doesn't matter," Genna Kastner said. "Not when we have hungry mouths to feed."

"I heard it was gold," another man said.

"Naw, more like silver or copper. If it were gold, we'd know," Ed said.

"It's uranium," Wyatt told them. "You know, the stuff they make nuclear weapons out of."

There was a pause as the group absorbed that information.

From the shadows of the back of the barn, a man stepped forward. "Uranium is used for more than just weaponry. It's used for electricity and fuel."

Pendleton. Figured the city slicker would be at the heart of this convention.

"The power from one kilogram of uranium is approximately equivalent to 100,000 kilograms of oil. Which means that mining for uranium has a lesser impact on the environment than drilling and mining for fossil fuels," Pendleton continued. "And unlike oil or gas, nuclear fuel is solid and immune to the environmental problems posed from spillage during transportation."

"No matter what spin you put on it, you can't tell me there aren't risks to mining uranium. Risks that would affect us and our children," Wyatt countered.

"No, I won't tell you there aren't risks. But aren't there risks in everything in life, Mr. Monroe?" Pendleton stepped fully into the circle. "What I will tell you is this—uranium is a naturally occurring element in soil, rocks and water. And yes, it's radioactive, but natural uranium's amount of radioactivity per gram is relatively low. The Degas Corporation takes every precaution to protect its workers, the public at large and the environment. We use a process called in situ leaching, with minimal surface disturbance and no tailings or waste rock. I have charts and reports that you can read that will prove to you that the Degas Corporation has only the best interests of the people of Lane County in mind during this process."

Wyatt held up a hand. "Right. Like you had my best interests at heart when you drilled on my land without my permission. I don't think so, Pendleton. I don't trust you, and I sure don't trust a corporation whose sole goal is to make money off the land."

"But aren't we all making money off the land?" Genna asked. "Our cattle and horses graze off the natural resources on our ranches. We cut our trees to sell as firewood. How is pulling a natural resource out of the ground any different from using the surface resources?"

"People won't end up with cancer from cutting down

a tree or from the animals eating the sagebrush." Millie Tipton spoke up for the first time.

Wyatt was grateful for her input. Apparently he wasn't the only one disturbed by the idea of uranium mining.

"The benefits outweigh the risk," Josh Freeman insisted. "I'm willing to take the risks on my land."

A chorus of "me, too" went around the circle.

"That's your choice," Wyatt said. "It's not mine."

"And I can respect that, Mr. Monroe," Pendleton said. "But to access some of your neighbors who'd like to accept our offer requires use of the roads cutting across your land."

Wyatt set his jaw. He stared at the faces looking back at him with expectation. He wanted to say no. He wanted to be selfish and make the decision that was best for him and his family. Yet he understood what his neighbors were saying. These were tough economic times. Granting access to the roads might be a compromise he could make. He'd have to pray about it. "I need to think on it."

That was as much of a commitment as he could make.

But the disquiet creeping through him like a thief in the night had him eyeing his neighbors with wary suspicion. Someone had tried to kill him. Had it been one of these people?

Yet here they all stood talking to him, reasonable and desperate. Desperate enough to do him bodily harm?

Or was there something more going on?

He wondered what Jackie would say, how she would feel about all of this. And he wondered when her opinions had become so important to him.

* * *

Jackie parked her uncle's truck behind Wyatt's rig. At least she'd found him. She let out a breath of relief. And apparently there was a party going on, judging by the number of other vehicles parked in the Dunns' large driveway. She placed a call to the sheriff with the news that she'd found Wyatt and told him about the change of venue. Sheriff Landers promised to head over right away. Pocketing her phone, she headed toward the house, but loud voices coming from the barn had her veering in that direction.

As she neared the door of the barn that was cracked open, she heard Wyatt say, "I need to think on it."

Then voices erupted, talking over each other.

"Come on, Wyatt. What's there to think about?" a man asked.

"Just say yes and be done with it," another man exclaimed.

She reached for the barn door handle, when the scuff of a shoe on the loose gravel of the walkway sent a shiver of alarm racing over her. Instantly, she reached for the weapon tucked inside the holster at her hip. A hand clamped over her mouth before she could turn around. The hard barrel of a gun jammed into her ribs.

"Don't struggle," a deep male voice hissed into her ear. "I'd hate to have to kill you."

She held still, assessing her attacker. Approximately six-four or so, with a strong grip. The fingers covering her mouth dug into her like sharp talons.

"Drop your weapon," the man said, his voice soft like a whisper in her ear. "Don't try anything or I *will* shoot you."

Weighing her options, she held the SIG out and dropped it at her feet. Her captor kicked the weapon aside until it was hidden in a clump of weeds. Yanking her backward, he propelled her away from the barn toward Uncle Carl's truck.

No way was she going anywhere with him. She jabbed her elbow back and connected with his ribs. He let out a satisfying grunt of pain. Using her heel, she stomped down on his instep.

"You've done it now," he muttered.

She fought harder. Twisting and turning, hoping to loosen his hold over her mouth so she could scream.

In her peripheral vision, she saw the hand holding the weapon swing toward her head. She tried to duck away. The butt of the gun rammed against her head, and pain exploded at her temple. The world winked out.

Jackie came to with a start. The musty smell of moldy earth and rust assaulted her senses. Her head throbbed. Her heart thundered in her chest. She blinked, taking in the dimly lit space. She was inside some sort of shed filled with yard tools and a workbench with a jagged table saw. She tried to rise, but duct tape had been wound across her chest and biceps, securing her to a metal chair. Her feet weren't bound. She kicked and struggled against the tape. She screamed with frustration.

"No one will hear you," a deep voice stated from somewhere to her right.

She whipped her head in that direction and immediately regretted the movement. She gritted her teeth against the ache in her head and stared at the man leaning against the wall. Piercing blue eyes regarded her steadily. Dark hair peeked out beneath a well-worn tan cowboy hat. His jaw line was firm and his shoulders broad. It was the man who had been with Boyd and Pendleton last night, out by the creek. Darrin Dunn.

"Why are you doing this?" she asked.

"I couldn't let you interrupt them." He pushed away from the wall and walked closer.

"What is this about?" she asked. "Are you working for the Degas Corporation?"

He scoffed. "Naw. But they're offering a lot of money for cooperation."

"The sheriff knows where I was going."

He shrugged. "No one saw you arrive. And no one saw you leave." He cocked his head for a moment, then took out a cell phone from his pocket. Her phone. "You're going to call your uncle and tell him you went into town."

She bent her elbows and waved her hands to show she couldn't lift a phone to her ear. "Sorry. No can do, unless you undo the tape."

"What's the number?"

She remained silent.

He walked to the workbench and picked up a Beretta 9 millimeter fitted with a sound suppressor. "You'll give me the number, or I'll shoot out your kneecap."

The menacing look in his eyes let her know he would do as he threatened. A wave of impotent fury hit her. She had no choice but to comply. She gave him the number. He dialed, put the device on speaker and held it close enough for her to speak into but not close enough for her to reach him with her limited mobility.

Her uncle answered on the first ring. "Did you find Wyatt?"

"Yes. He's fine." At least, she prayed he was. "I'm heading into town."

"Town?"

"Yes. I need some things."

"Oh. Okay." Doubt and confusion laced each word. "Well, let me ask Penny if there's anything you could pick up for her. You know she hates to go into town."

Darrin shook his head.

Jackie grimaced. "Uh, I'll have to call back. Gotta go."

Darrin powered the phone off and stuffed it into his pocket.

"You can't keep me here."

He shrugged. "It shouldn't be long. Only until Monroe signs the papers."

She was supposed to believe he'd let her go? "And if he doesn't?"

He gave a smug smile. "Oh, he will once he learns we have you."

"You want to use me as leverage?" She let out a dry laugh. Unbelievable. The guy was out of his mind. Though knowing Wyatt, he'd feel responsible for her capture and would do whatever he needed to rescue her. But she had to make Darrin believe otherwise. "Dude, Wyatt's not going to care one way or the other. We've only just met. We hardly know each other."

"Didn't look that way to me." He wagged his dark eyebrows. "The way you two were kissing, I'd say there's something going on."

Her stomach tightened. He'd seen that? Totally

creeped out, she shivered and raised a leg to rest her ankle on her knee; her second weapon was beneath her pant leg, and she wanted it close. The familiar feel of the piece's weight in the holster gave her a measure of peace. Now if she could only get to it.

She covered her calf with her hand. "It was one kiss that meant nothing." And meant everything. At least to her.

"You're not a very good liar," he stated. "I know Wyatt. He doesn't mess around with anyone. Every single female within a hundred-mile radius has been after him since his wife died. You're the first to catch his fancy. I say he'll care and do what he needs to do."

"Or what?" she shot back. "You're going to kill me either way, aren't you? Just like you tried to kill Wyatt the other day when you shot at his truck."

Darrin scoffed. "If I had wanted either of you dead, you'd be dead."

She believed him. There was something very dangerous about this man. "You killed George, though, didn't you?"

Darrin's mouth tightened, and he moved toward the workbench. Turing his back to her, he rummaged around the table.

Keeping her eye on his back, she eased her hand beneath her pant leg.

He whipped around, the gun aimed at her head. "Raise your hands," he snapped.

Frustration pulsed in her veins. She lifted her hands, palm up. "Sorry, had an itch."

He approached. She braced herself. He kicked her foot off her knee.

Tires on the dirt outside the shed sent her captor scurrying toward the door.

"Help! Someone help me!" she screamed, hoping to alert whoever was out there, praying it was a friend and not a foe.

Darrin moved swiftly to the wall and pressed his back next to the door, just as it slid open.

Boyd Dunn stepped inside. He stopped short when he saw Jackie. Confusion twisted his face. "Darrin, what's going on?"

She'd been right. Her assailant was Darrin Dunn. "Help me," she pleaded. "Your brother's crazy."

Boyd grinned. "Yes, ma'am, he is that. On every day that ends with a *y*."

Darrin pushed away from the wall. "Well, did he sign?"

Boyd shook his head as his gaze flicked over her. "No. What's she doing here?"

"I found her snooping around the barn. I didn't want her mess'n' anything up."

"Now what?" Boyd asked, turning toward his brother. "The old man will not be happy about this."

"You let me worry about him. Is Monroe still at the house?"

Boyd shrugged. "Was when I left." Jutting his chin in her direction, he asked, "What'ya gonna do with her?"

"Monroe will sign when he learns we have his ladylove," Darrin stated.

Boyd seemed to think that over. "Maybe. Maybe not. He killed his wife. So what makes you think he'll care about this one?"

A dark light entered Darrin's blue eyes. Foreboding

skated over Jackie, leaving a trail of chills in its wake. "Then we'll take what he does care about."

"Oh, yeah, what's that?"

"His kid."

Jackie's heart sank. Failure ripped through her. Gabby was in danger now, too. Wyatt would never forgive her if anything happened to his daughter. She'd never forgive herself.

FIFTEEN

Wyatt's eyebrows rose when Sheriff Landers walked into the barn. What was his stepfather doing here?

"What's the meaning of this?" Landers pushed his way into the circle and came to a halt beside Wyatt.

"A little friendly meeting, Sheriff. Nothing to get worked up about," Frank Dunn stated. "Wyatt came of his own free will."

Landers met Wyatt's gaze. Wyatt nodded. Yes, he'd come of his own accord. He had a feeling if Landers hadn't shown up, these people wouldn't have let Wyatt leave. At least without signing the papers laid across the top of a nearby oak barrel. But he didn't want to sign those papers, so for the first time in his life he took advantage of the fact that his stepfather was the law in this town. "I was just leaving. Walk me out, Sheriff."

Landers's eyebrows twitched. "Good. Let's go."

They left the barn and headed toward where the sheriff's cruiser sat parked behind Wyatt's rig. "What was that all about?"

"A plea to change my mind about taking the Degas offer."

"And?"

Wyatt sighed. "I'm still thinking."

"You better check in at home," Landers said as they halted beside his car. "Ms. Blain and her relatives were pretty upset that you'd taken off."

He'd just bet. He should have at least told Carl he was headed to the Dunn ranch. But at least Jackie was there watching over Gabby. "How did you find me?"

Landers gave him a wry look. "How do you think?"

"Jackie," Wyatt stated. A pressure built in his chest. She'd been worried enough about him to call the sheriff.

"Righto. She followed a goose chase out to the Freeman ranch, but eventually figured you'd headed here." He frowned. "She said she was heading this way."

Wyatt frowned, too. He should have known she wouldn't stay put. "She must have realized I wasn't in any danger and went back to the ranch," he reasoned, though a sense of uneasiness crept over him. He pulled out his cell phone and dialed Jackie's number. It went straight to voice mail. Wyatt called Carl Kirk.

After the first ring, Carl answered. "You're safe?"

"Yeah. No worries. Where's Jackie?"

"She called, said she'd found you and that you were all right. She was heading to town for something."

Odd that she didn't check in with him since she'd gone through all the trouble of tracking him down. But then again, it wasn't as if he was her responsibility, even if she said she wanted to be his self-appointed bodyguard. Yet...he couldn't shake the strange sense of foreboding winding its way through him. "Tell Gabby I'm on my way home."

"Will do," Carl said. "And, Wyatt, we're glad you're all right."

Affection for the older couple spread a warm path through his chest. "Thanks."

He hung up and relayed what he'd been told to Landers.

"Would you mind following me to the house?" Landers asked. "Your mother really needs some face time with you."

Anxiety kicked up its heels. "Is Mom okay?"

"She's fine. She'd be better if she could talk to you. It would ease her mind to know firsthand how you're doing."

Staring into his stepfather's eyes, Wyatt saw concern and tenderness directed at him. Jackie's words about Craig caring echoed in his head. He had thought she was mistaken, but now he realized she'd been right. His stepfather did care about him.

"I know you and I haven't had the best relationship," Landers said, his voice low and full of emotion. "I can never replace your father. I understand that. But I want you to understand, this anger you harbor toward your mother is undeserved. She tried hard with your dad. You have no idea what he put her through."

Wyatt stiffened. Fury spread through his chest like lava flowing from the mound of bitterness lodged somewhere near his heart and wiped away the moment of kinship he'd been feeling. "She left my dad for you. There's not much more for me to know."

"There's a lot more." Craig's voice shook with suppressed rage. "Your father was an abusive drunk long before she left him. He wouldn't get help. Your mother left him hoping he'd realize how bad it had gotten and change. But he didn't." Craig stepped closer until he was in Wyatt's face, his eyes narrowed. "And for the record, your mom and I didn't start dating until six months after their divorce was final."

The stunning revelation knocked Wyatt back on his heels. "That's not what my dad said."

"Your dad wanted to use you as a way to hurt your mom. And he succeeded, didn't he?"

Shaking his head, Wyatt tried to deny what Craig said. But deep inside, the truth stirred like a bear awakening after a long winter sleep. Memories, long buried, surfaced. The fights before his mom left. Images of his dad drunk and snarling at Mom, at him. The way his dad had blamed his mom for everything, even when the ranch was losing money. Wyatt hadn't learned to be a businessman from his father, not really. His dad tried to teach him, but Dad had been too intoxicated to make much sense. But he'd been his dad. Wyatt had craved his attention. And now he realized, as guilt swamped him, that he'd turned his back on his mother because of lies and false beliefs.

"Why didn't she ever tell me this?" Wyatt asked.

Craig's anger faded, and compassion softened his expression. "She didn't want to hurt you."

But he'd hurt her. Time and again.

Now he realized his view of her had been skewed. Tainted.

Jackie's image rose in his mind. She would tell him to get over himself. To let go of the past and make amends.

God's plan is better than any we could ever come up with.

What plan did God have for Wyatt?

Jackie believed God had a plan for her. Jackie, who

had every right to be bitter and hardened after what her fiancé had done, was loving and caring and so full of life. She made Wyatt want to be a better man. And a better man would do his best to repair his relationship with his mother.

"I'll come to the house," he said.

Landers gave a satisfied nod and climbed into his car. As Wyatt followed Landers, he checked his cell phone. He had two missed calls. He listened to the messages. One from Carl wanting to know if he was okay. And one from Jackie. Her voice sounded stressed. No doubt upset that he'd taken off without her.

But he couldn't help the spurt of hope that maybe her concern stemmed from more than her need to act as his bodyguard. He wanted her to care about him. As a man—a man who cared about her. Warmth spread through his chest as images of Jackie played across his mind. Wild curls, impish face so full of life. Her laugh melted his heart. Okay, he cared. More than he should or wanted to. But he did. Didn't mean he'd act on it.

He brought his truck to a halt in front of Landers's single-story house on the outskirts of town in one of the more modern residential neighborhoods that had sprung up over the past decade or so.

A white picket fence surrounded a well-kept yard with a lush lawn and an array of colorful blossoms. Wyatt entered the house behind Landers and slowly closed the door. The scent of fried chicken permeated the air and made Wyatt's stomach rumble. He missed his mother's cooking. He did okay for himself and Gabby, but there was nothing like his mother's chicken. Shaking off the nostalgia clogging his throat, he stepped fully into the living room. The place hadn't changed much over the years. Well lived in, with furniture in a deep red fabric, pictures of Gabby hanging on the walls and a television in the corner.

His mother entered from the kitchen, an apron covering her jeans and plaid shirt. Her short dark hair curled about her face, and her smile was so happy and full of love and directed at him. It melted the coldness around his heart.

He opened his arms. "Mom."

She flew to him and hugged him tight. "I could hardly believe it when Craig called to say you were stopping by. I can't tell you how happy it makes me."

Guilt twisted him up inside. "Sorry, Mom."

She pulled back to look up at him. Her dark eyes never missed anything. "No apologies. It's been a trying time for you. Ever since…"

She winced slightly and withdrew from him. He wasn't sure if she were referring to George's murder or Dina's death. Truth be told, times had been trying way before either of those two events had slammed into his life. But why rub at old wounds? "I just wanted to stop in and let you know I'm okay. Everything is okay. Gabby's okay. We're all okay."

But even to his own ears, the words sounded hollow. He'd thought he was doing well. Had convinced himself his world was complete with just him and Gabby. That was before a certain curly-haired, blue-eyed blonde had rushed to his defense in the jailhouse and inserted herself into his life. An ache throbbed beneath his breastbone. He absently rubbed over the spot.

"Please tell me you'll stay for supper," his mother said.

He shook his head. "I need to get home to Gabby."

"I'm sure Carl and Penny have already fed her," Mom insisted. "And you need to eat. It won't take long. I have mashed potatoes, green beans and fried chicken."

His stomach grumbled again. It was hard to pass up his mother's food. "I'll eat. But I can't stay long."

She threaded her arm through his and pulled him into the kitchen. Craig was setting the table. Three place settings. Interesting. Craig had been confident Mom would talk him into staying.

"Wash your hands," Mom instructed Wyatt. With a beaming smile, she said to Craig, "Set him a place."

Craig nodded. "Already done."

Wyatt washed up and then sat in his old spot. For a moment he was transported back in time to high school, when his mother had insisted he sit at the table for dinner with them on Sundays. He'd been sullen, hurt and angry and had made his displeasure known quite loudly. Shame for his behavior itched like a tick burrowing in. He owed his mother an apology. He didn't know where to begin.

His mother sat on his right, and his stepfather across from him.

"Craig, would you say grace?" Mom asked.

"My pleasure," Craig said with a loving smile at his wife.

Wyatt's heart squeezed tight. Why had he never seen how much these two loved each other? Too self-absorbed. Too self-centered. Too hurt to look beyond his own pain.

"Dear Lord, thank You for this meal we're about to

receive, and thank You for the family we have here to-night."

Wyatt blinked back the burning in his eyes. Family. He'd missed out because he'd been so full of pride and anger. It had to stop. He was letting Gabby down by keeping a wall between him and his mother and step-father.

"Thank You, Father God. Amen," Craig finished.

"Amen," Wyatt echoed. He slid his hand over his mother's. "Mom, I owe you an apology. For so many things. For being such a pain growing up, for staying away."

She gripped his hand. "It's all in the past. What matters is you're here now."

"I didn't kill Dina, Mom." The words broke from him before he could hold them back.

"Oh, Wyatt, I know you didn't."

"But you asked if I did. I thought maybe you thought... I mean, you guys were so close, I thought you were choosing her."

Mom's face softened. "I liked Dina. We *were* close. But only because she was your wife. I wanted your marriage to work out. She needed a place to go to give you room."

He withdrew his hand as shame infused him. "She shouldn't have had to seek refuge. I should have been a better man. Better husband."

"I don't think she made it easy on you," Mom said. "She was a difficult woman. Spoiled, in fact. And very selfish."

Wyatt cocked his head. "What?"

Mom shrugged. "She wanted things a certain way.

Her way. She wasn't interested in learning how to be a rancher's wife. She wanted to be taken care of, not have to take care of others."

Wyatt swallowed back his surprise. He hadn't known anyone else had seen that about her. His mind replayed the night she died. He spoke as the memories rushed in. "We'd been fighting the night she died. Again. Because she didn't like having to spend her days alone. She didn't like how much time I spent working on the ranch. She wanted to go someplace where I could get a normal nine-to-five type of job. I remembered saying she knew what she was getting into when we married. I never lied to her about my life or about what life on the ranch would be like." He shook his head. "Then she'd said she was leaving and taking Gabby."

He heard his mom's small gasp.

Wyatt looked down at his plate. The fried chicken was getting cold. But his appetite was gone. "She said she didn't even know if Gabby was mine."

"That's ridiculous," Mom stated firmly. "Of course she's yours. Gabby has your nose and your spirit."

"This is what you've been hiding," Craig said softly.

Wyatt met his gaze. "Yes. I was afraid if you knew she'd been having an affair, it would make me seem more guilty."

"Oh, no," Mom said. "I didn't think it had gotten to that stage."

Wyatt turned his gaze to his mother. "What do you mean?"

"I knew she'd become friendly with someone, but when I confronted her, she'd said they were only friends."

Wyatt sucked in a sharp breath. His chest contracted

painfully as he asked, "Who? Who was she becoming friendly with?"

"Boyd Dunn."

Hurt burrowed in deep. Some small part of him had always wanted to believe she had been lying, lashing out only to hurt him. Apparently she hadn't lied. It was one thing to think his wife had betrayed him with a nameless, faceless man. But now he knew. She'd been having an affair with Boyd Dunn.

And Gabby might not be his biological child. Did Wyatt have the right to keep Gabby's paternity a secret?

Jackie's words came back to him. *Secrets have a way of eating at a person until they crumble.*

He didn't want to crumble beneath the weight of any secret.

He hated the secrets that Dina had kept. And he didn't want to perpetuate a tangle of lies. He wanted to set a good example for Gabby.

His foundation was built on faith. Whatever the truth was, he and Gabby would survive. But he realized now that he didn't have a choice. Tomorrow he'd start the process to find out if Gabby was truly his child.

Because no matter what, she would always be his precious little girl.

The ring of his cell phone jarred him out of his thoughts. "Excuse me," he said to his mother as he reached for the phone in his pocket.

"Mr. Monroe?" an unfamiliar female voice asked.

"Yes, this is Wyatt Monroe."

"This is Simone Walker from Trent Associates. I work with Jackie Blain," the woman said. Her voice held a taut note of concern.

"Jackie's spoken of you. What can I do for you?"

"Have you seen or heard from Jackie in the past few hours?"

"No." Apprehension spread across him like ice water. A chill ran down his spine. The sense of foreboding reared again. "Is there something wrong?"

"I don't know. Her phone has been turned off. She never turns her phone off, and I know she'd never let it die. She was looking for you when I last spoke to her. She had me run your last few calls on your cell phone," Simone said. "She was upset when I told her you'd called someone named Frank Dunn."

Wyatt blinked. Jackie *had* gone to a lot of trouble to find him. Then why didn't she show up at the Dunns'? Carl said she'd gone into town for something. He'd thought that was odd. Where was she?

He promised Ms. Walker he'd find Jackie. Then he called the Kirks. The phone just rang.

Dread squeezed the breath from his lungs in a forceful vise. Something was wrong. Jackie was in trouble. A deep-seated knowledge that his daughter was in danger threatened to choke the air from his body.

He explained the situation to Craig and he tried to keep the panic at bay.

"You head to the ranch," Craig instructed. "I'll go into town and see if I can find Ms. Blain."

Grateful for his stepfather's help, Wyatt ran for his truck.

"I'm coming with you," his mother said and jumped in before he could protest. "Gabby's my granddaughter."

The whole drive to the ranch, Wyatt prayed. Prayed that he was overreacting, that he'd find Gabby safe and sound, curled up with Penny and Carl on the couch watching some animated movie. He prayed that Jackie was safe and already back at the ranch.

As Wyatt drove up to the house, apprehension slithered over his flesh like a prairie rattlesnake. The main house was dark, as was the Kirks' home. He brought the truck to a halt, jumped out and ran for the Kirks' front door. He heard the frantic barking of Jackie's dog somewhere inside. Rapping his knuckles on the wood, he tried to keep the anxiety filling him from sending him into a panic.

No one answered. He knocked again, hard, then shouted, "Penny? Carl? Open up."

Nothing. With panic racing through his veins, he rammed his shoulder against the door and burst into the living room. He found the light switch and flipped it.

Penny Kirk sat in a chair with her feet and hands bound, a rag stuffed in her mouth. Her wide eyes stared at him with relief and fear. A tear rolled down her cheek. His mother let out a gasp of horror.

Terror flooded Wyatt. He rushed to her side and took out the rag. "What happened? Where's Gabby?"

"He took her," Penny said, her voice hoarse and raspy.

"Who took my baby?"

"Boyd Dunn."

A fist of fury slammed into his gut. If he hurt his little girl…there was nothing that would keep Wyatt from tearing the man limb from limb.

Staggering beneath the weight of fear pressing down on him, he asked, "Where's Carl? Jackie?"

Penny shook her head. Tears slipped down her cheeks.

"Carl was in the back of the house when Boyd came in. Jackie hasn't returned from town."

"I've got this," his mother said as she worked at the bonds holding Penny to the chair. "Go. Find Carl."

Barely keeping his control, Wyatt ran to the kitchen and found Carl unconscious on the floor. Blood trickled from a gash on his forehead. Wyatt checked his pulse. He was alive.

"Thank You, Jesus," Wyatt breathed out and then grabbed the phone to call 911. The dispatcher promised an ambulance was on its way and that the sheriff would be informed. His mother and Penny crowded around Carl. Penny rocked with sobs, while his mother held her.

Torn between his need to find his daughter and Jackie and feeling obligated to stay put, Wyatt paced the kitchen.

"What are you doing? Go find Gabby," his mother insisted.

Grateful to be given the order, he ran from the house and took off in his truck toward the Dunn ranch. He had a sinking feeling in the pit of his stomach that Jackie was in danger, too.

Fear clutched at him with greedy fingers. He couldn't take it if anything happened to Gabby or Jackie. He pressed down hard on the gas and raced toward the unknown.

"Lord, please protect Gabby and Jackie, the two people I love most in this world. Keep them safe. Let them know I'm coming."

SIXTEEN

"Why did you kill George?" Jackie asked Darrin Dunn. She surreptitiously worked to loosen the duct tape trapping her to the chair. She swallowed around a lump of frustration and bit back a sigh. She'd made little progress so far. And that worried her.

The strong tape pulled taut around her torso and stuck like glue. She was thankful he hadn't put any across her mouth. Feeling helpless and vulnerable in the chair was bad enough. Being muzzled, unable to speak or breathe without effort, would have driven her crazy.

She repeated her question, careful to keep her growing desperation from sounding in her voice.

Darrin didn't lift his gaze from the carving in his hands or acknowledge her in any way. For the past hour he'd been ignoring her questions. He sat on a workbench, whittling a chunk of wood with a large hunting knife. She watched the way his hands deftly handled the blade. Here was a man who knew how to work with a sharp instrument. A man who had stabbed George to death?

Part of her didn't want to know the answer, because if the answer was yes, he would have no qualms about killing her the same way.

She gave the tape another tug. It wouldn't give.

How long would he wait for his brother to return with Gabby before he grew impatient? And then what would this man do?

She sent up a prayer that Wyatt had already returned to the ranch. He'd never let Boyd do anything to Gabby. But who knew what Boyd had planned? Both of the brothers were a bit unhinged.

He might burn down the barn or the house this time and hope to snatch Gabby in the chaos. But Jackie couldn't think about that. She had to trust that God would keep them safe. She had to concentrate on the here and now. She had to escape.

"Did George find out about the uranium? Is that why you killed him? He was going to tell, wasn't he?" She would keep pestering him, hoping to get some of her questions answered. "Why did you burn down the feed shed and let Alexander loose?"

Darrin continued to whittle away, piling slivers of wood on the floor at his feet, offering nothing. She might as well be alone and talking to herself. Maybe a good thing, given the situation.

With his general resemblance to Wyatt, she would stake her reputation on the fact that Darrin Dunn was the man who'd led George away from the Whiskey Saloon and killed him. And tried to frame Wyatt for the murder.

The man was a cold-blooded killer, but no one knew that except her. And she might be his next victim.

Frustration pounded at her temples. The waiting was nearly as maddening as being imprisoned in this awful outbuilding. The chilled air contributed to the numbness in her limbs. She wanted to act, to lash out, but she couldn't move. She flexed her stiff fingers, wishing she could reach the weapon inside her boot.

The door to the toolshed slid open. Jackie jerked her gaze away from Darrin. Boyd walked in, carrying a whimpering Gabby in his arms like a sack of potatoes.

Jackie's breath stalled. "Gabby!"

Gabby's eyes widened. She squirmed ferociously in Boyd's arms. "Jackie!"

"Do not hurt her!" Jackie exploded as fury poured into her veins. She pulled against her restraints. The tape bit into her arms through her jacket. She didn't care. Her only concern was for Gabby. If anything happened to her... The thought made it difficult to breathe.

Boyd frowned. "I wouldn't hurt a kid. She's fine."

He set Gabby on her feet. She immediately ran to Jackie's side and clung to her. Tears streamed down the child's face. Everything inside Jackie wanted to pull the little girl into her arms, but she couldn't. She did what she could to soothe Gabby. Jackie tried to nuzzle her with her cheek. "Shh, it's okay, sweetie. You're okay."

Darrin set the wood aside, sheathed his knife inside his cowboy boot and then picked up his handgun from the workbench. He crossed to his brother and handed him the gun. "You watch them. I'll go make sure Monroe signs the papers."

Jackie noticed the way Boyd stiffened as he gripped the gun. The man obviously wasn't comfortable with the piece. She could take advantage of that as long as Gabby wouldn't be in the line of fire.

As soon as Darrin left, Jackie said, "Boyd, please take this tape off so I can comfort Gabby." She had to convince him, not only for Gabby, but also for herself. For Wyatt. She couldn't let him down.

He shook his head. "Naw. Better not. Darrin would get angry. He's not nice when he's angry."

"He won't know. Please," she said. "Look at her. She's terrified."

As if on cue, Gabby wailed. The sound was plaintive and heartbreaking.

"I don't know."

The indecision in his eyes gave her hope. "Come on, she's a kid. You don't want to do this." She remembered the way the two brothers argued. Darrin had wanted Boyd to stay while he went to kidnap Gabby, but Boyd had insisted he'd do it. "You don't want to hurt Gabby. That's why you offered to go instead of letting your brother. Right? Because you know he'd hurt her."

Boyd stared at Gabby. "She looks just like Dina."

The sad, longing note in his voice sent surprise sliding through Jackie. Boyd and Dina? Jackie remembered the passionate way he'd accused Wyatt of killing Dina. At the time she'd wondered if he'd been related to Dina in some way. Now she understood. He'd loved her. Dina's words to Wyatt rang in her head. "Could Gabby be yours? Were you and Dina…together?"

He frowned and flushed a deep red. "We never… She wasn't… We didn't."

Jackie was glad to hear that. "But you did love Dina, right?"

"Yes!" A shadow of pain crossed his face. "She deserved so much more than Wyatt Monroe. She was a sweet, beautiful lady. She was withering away on the ranch. We were going to run off together. She was going to divorce Wyatt. We were going to start a new life somewhere else. But then he…" The unspoken accusation hung in the air.

"If you truly loved Dina, then think of what she'd want you to do. Dina wouldn't want Gabby to be scared. Think of Dina. She would want you to let me loose to comfort her baby."

Boyd blinked. "I can take care of Dina." He gave himself a shake. "Dina's baby." He moved closer. Gabby shrieked and ducked under the chair, curling into a ball.

He frowned. "Why's she doing that?"

Holding on to her patience by a thin thread, Jackie kept her voice gentle, as if she were talking to a child. "She's scared. Boyd, you're scaring her. Please, let me loose. You have a gun." She flicked her chin toward his hand where, thankfully, he didn't have a finger on the trigger. "I'm not going to try anything."

He glanced down at his hand as if suddenly remembering he held the weapon. "That's right. I've got the power."

Emboldened by his own statement, he moved to the workbench and rummaged around until he found a small utility knife. When he came back to her side, he said, "Don't try anything funny or I'll shoot *you*."

"I wouldn't dream of it," she answered, hoping God would forgive her for the lie if she did do something.

He used the knife to cut through the tape. Then he backed up, the gun aimed at her chest. Jackie crouched down to help Gabby crawl out from under the chair. She wrapped her arms around Jackie's neck and her legs around her waist. Jackie turned so her back faced Boyd. The warmth of the child pressed against her filled her with a poignant need. A yearning she'd tried to keep locked away but that had surged to the forefront of her heart since she'd come to the ranch. Since she'd met Gabby. And Wyatt.

Jackie stroked Gabby's red curly hair. Her heart welled with love and a protectiveness that went beyond anything she'd ever felt before. This was what she wanted—needed.

Loud, angry male voices coming from outside filled the shed. Glancing toward the door, Jackie tightened her hold on Gabby.

Boyd's attention was riveted to the commotion.

Jackie took the opportunity to rush Gabby to the workbench. "Hide," she whispered to Gabby. "Quick."

Gabby clung to her for a second then slipped from her arms, scrambled beneath the workbench and wedged herself into a corner behind a large toolbox. While crouched down, Jackie withdrew her weapon from the holster at her ankle and tucked it into her jacket pocket.

"Hey! What are you doing?"

Jackie straightened, keeping her hand in her pocket and her finger on the trigger, and turned slowly toward Boyd.

"Did you kill George?" she asked, hoping to throw him off balance.

"What? No. Not me. That was Darrin's doing."

His answer confirmed what she'd already guessed.

He gestured with the gun. "Come away from there." He scowled with confusion lighting his eyes. "Where's the kid?"

"But you burned down the shed," she said, leaving his question unanswered.

He moved forward and bent down to peer under the bench.

"Hey!" Jackie said. "Look at me. I have questions for you."

She edged away from the workbench, drawing Boyd's aim away from Gabby. If he did fire, she didn't want Gabby to be inadvertently hit. "When did you meet Dina? How did you fall in love?"

He jerked upright.

The voices outside grew louder, closer. Jackie thought for a moment that she heard Wyatt's voice. Not sure if she should be hopeful or scared, she inched farther from the workbench and closer to Boyd.

Hoping to keep him distracted, she peppered him with more questions. "Why did you let Alexander loose? What did you hope to gain? When did you realize there was uranium on the land? Does Pendleton know you've kidnapped me and Gabby?"

He glanced her way, blinking as if remembering she was there. "I didn't mean to let him loose. I was going to take him, but he broke away and ran."

The door slid open, and Boyd jumped back. Jackie braced herself—then Wyatt stormed inside. Hope shot through her, until she realized he had his hands raised and his features set in stone. Plus he was followed by Frank Dunn, who also had his hands held high. Worry chomped through her. What?

Darrin Dunn filed in behind them, holding a large-caliber tactical rifle. The rifle he'd used to shoot out the tire on her rented SUV.

Apparently Darrin was more unhinged than she'd

first guessed. Why was he aiming at his own father? Jackie's gut clenched with dread.

She hoped Gabby would stay hidden when she realized Wyatt was here.

"Boyd!" Darrin barked. "What have you done?"

"Me?" Boyd lowered his weapon. "What are you doing? Why did you bring Dad into this?"

Darrin didn't answer. But the hatred in his dark eyes didn't bode well for any of them.

Jackie met Wyatt's anxious gaze. He mouthed, *Gabby.* She wanted to reassure him, but Darrin shifted, drawing her attention. The guy was twitchy. There was no telling what he would do. She needed a way to control this situation. But how?

Lord, help me here. I need a plan.

Wyatt stared at Jackie as a wave of relief that she was alive and well crashed over him, making his knees buckle, but he stayed upright. His heart hiccuped and willed her to tell him about Gabby. Fear for his child ate away at his composure. He was holding back panic by a thin thread. His daughter had to be all right. Safe. *Please.*

For a moment Jackie stared back, her blue eyes wide and intent. Then she was rushing to him, throwing her arms around him and spinning him away from Darrin.

"Hey!" Darrin yelled.

"She's safe," Jackie whispered quickly.

Confused by her behavior, yet thankful to know his daughter was okay, he held her tight. Then she turned in his arms and he realized what she'd done. She'd put herself in the line of fire. *No!*

Keeping his hand on her shoulder, he stepped to her side. He wouldn't hide behind anyone, least of all the woman he loved. The realization rocked him to the core, but now was not the time to deal with the ramifications. Not when a madman had a weapon pointed at them. They needed a distraction. Something to stall him until Craig and his men could arrive.

"Why are you doing this, Darrin?" Wyatt asked.

"Son, put the rifle down." Frank Dunn drew his son's attention.

"Not until he signs those papers."

Wyatt heard a noise behind him. He glanced back. Gabby was peeking out at him from the workbench. His breath caught. He wanted to run to her, but he also didn't want to draw attention to her. He waved her back with his hand.

"I don't have them here." Frank spread his hands wide. "This is not the way to do this, son."

"He won't sign them unless we make him," Darrin said.

"Think about what you're doing," Frank said. "Son, I don't want this. Your mother, bless her soul, would not want this."

Darrin trained the rifle on his father. The loathing twisting his face made Wyatt's blood run cold.

"I don't care what she'd want," he snarled.

"Darrin, come on, let Dad go," Boyd said. "This isn't right."

Darrin swung the tip of the rifle to Boyd. "You. You were always the favorite."

The sound of Darrin's laughter raised the fine hairs at the back of Wyatt's neck. The man was coming unglued right before their eyes. And the two most important people in his life were here. He couldn't let anything happen to them.

Jackie shifted her stance and jammed her hand into her pocket.

"That's not fair," Boyd whined. "It's not my fault."

"No, it was her fault," Darrin snapped.

Wyatt didn't know who they referred to. He could only guess Darrin meant his mother. It didn't make sense.

Frank stepped closer. "This isn't the time or place for this, Darrin."

A sneer spread across Darrin's face. "Of course it is, Daddy."

The way he drew out the moniker with such disgust confused Wyatt. He shared a puzzled glance with Jackie. What was going on? The family drama playing out had nothing to do with him and Jackie, yet they were held captive as unwilling spectators. But at any moment Darrin's focus could once again turn to him and Jackie. Who knew what he'd do then?

Darrin narrowed his eyes on his father. "Why don't you tell my brother about me?"

"What about you?" Boyd asked, clearly as confused as Wyatt and Jackie.

"Not you," Darrin shot back. He swung the rifle toward Wyatt. "Him."

What? Wyatt tried to make sense of what Darrin was saying. His brother?

"That's right," Darrin sneered. "You and me. We have the same daddy."

Shock siphoned the blood from Wyatt's brain. "That's

not true." Wyatt looked at Frank to deny the words, but the grim resignation on the old man's face hit Wyatt like a hoof to the abdomen. His father and Mrs. Dunn? "When? How could this be?"

"Yeah, Daddy. How could this be?" Darrin demanded.

Frank seemed to age right before Wyatt's eyes. His shoulders drooped. Haggard lines deepened in his face. "The summer before Marilyn and I married, she and Emerson had been involved. But she left him for me. It wasn't until after our wedding that she realized she was already pregnant. I loved her," Frank stated. He turned to his eldest child. "And I loved you. It didn't matter that you weren't my biological child."

"Yeah, right," Darrin spat out. "You always treated us differently. You babied him. Me? You sent me away as soon as you could."

Reeling from this revelation, Wyatt asked, "When did you find out?"

"Oh, I've known for years." Darrin's lip curled in a snarl. "I was injured during my tour in the Middle East. I needed a blood transfusion. Found out I'm type A." His gaze zeroed in on Frank. "My mother was type O. And guess what?" He smirked and pointed a finger at Frank. "So is he. It's biologically impossible for him to be my father."

Wyatt sucked in a stunned breath. His father was type A. Just like Wyatt.

"Why do you think it was Mr. Monroe?" Jackie asked.

Darrin scoffed. "Look at us, lady. Don't you see it?"

Feeling sick, Wyatt did see. They had the same stature, the same shape to their face as Emerson Monroe.

The wail of a siren rising on the night breeze shuddered through Wyatt.

Darrin cocked his head and listened, then narrowed his gaze on Wyatt. "Sounds like your stepdaddy's coming. This will be a regular family reunion."

"He won't be alone," Wyatt said between clenched teeth.

"But he'll be too late," Darrin countered, raising the rifle to his shoulder.

The oxygen in the shed disappeared as time slowed. His lungs seizing with horror, Wyatt knew that at any second his life could end. His child would be orphaned. He'd never have the opportunity to tell Jackie how he felt. *Dear Lord, please.*

The loud retort of a gun blast trembled through the air. Wyatt flinched. But felt no pain.

Darrin jerked back. A bright red stain spread across his shoulder, down the front of his blue shirt. The rifle slipped from his hands and landed with a clatter on the floor.

For a stunned moment, no one else moved.

Darrin slowly sank to the ground and toppled over, groaning in pain.

Wyatt drew in air and filled his lungs as relief oozed through his veins.

Frank dropped to his knees beside his fallen son and pressed his hands over the gunshot wound. Boyd stared, slack jawed at his brother and father.

In a swift move, Jackie disarmed Boyd. He didn't even seem to notice.

Wyatt noted the black, burned hole marring the right pocket of her jacket. Not taking the time to register what had happened, he rushed to the workbench. His only thought was to have his daughter safe in his arms.

"It's okay, Gabby. You can come out now," he said, his voice thick with love and fear and gratitude. She climbed out from beneath the bench and launched herself into his arms. He checked her for injuries. "Are you hurt?"

"No, Daddy."

He kissed her head, her cheek. Gabby lifted her tear-filled eyes. "Jackie?"

"I'm here, baby," Jackie said, coming to their side.

Slipping his arm around her shoulders and drawing her close was the most natural thing to do. It felt right, complete. Gabby reached out to wrap one arm around Jackie's neck while still clinging to Wyatt.

In that moment, Wyatt knew what he wanted more than anything else in life. The three of them to be a family. For Jackie to become his wife and the mother of his children. Yes, he wanted more children. With her.

A rightness settled over his heart.

But how could he ask her to stay on the ranch? To give up the life of action and adventure she had built for herself?

A pain so deep sliced through him. He couldn't.

Nor could he uproot Gabby from the only home she'd ever known and move her to Boston. The ranch was his legacy to his daughter.

He was a rancher, not a city slicker. He wouldn't replay the same scenario he'd had with Dina. Not with Jackie. It wouldn't be fair to him, Jackie or Gabby.

He buried his face in his daughter's hair to conceal the anguish rushing through him. *Lord, how do I resolve this situation? How do I let Jackie go?*

Jackie rested her head against Wyatt's shoulder as uniformed officers flooded the shed. She glanced up to see Wyatt meet the sheriff's gaze and nod. Relief flooded Craig Landers's pale face. Why Wyatt ever thought his stepfather didn't care about him was beyond her. The sheriff loved his stepson and his step-grandchild something fierce.

She guessed when someone convinced themselves things were one way, it was hard to see the truth. Just as she had in thinking that she could give up being a law officer to be a bodyguard and be content.

An officer handcuffed Boyd and led him out. Frank sat back on his haunches and sobbed as the EMTs arrived and worked on Darrin as he lay bleeding on the concrete floor. She'd hit him in the shoulder, a shot meant to stop, not kill.

She'd practiced that hip shot often at the shooting range, but she had never had an occasion to use it in real life.

Now she could say with truth that she could shoot from the hip like a real-life cowboy.

She snuggled closer to the very real cowboy at her side, grateful for his arm around her, holding her tight. It made her heart ache to think she'd be leaving soon now that he was no longer a target. She'd done her job; now it was time to say goodbye. Best to make a clean break as soon as possible—less painful that way.

She shifted away from Wyatt and immediately missed

his embrace. She would have to get used to life without him. And Gabby. The thought lodged a knot beneath her breastbone. She ignored it.

"Darrin's got a knife inside his left boot," Jackie informed the sheriff.

Landers nodded and bent to fish the blade from Darrin's boot.

"Let's get out of here," Wyatt said, putting a hand on the small of Jackie's back and propelling her toward the shed door.

"Ms. Blain?" Craig called out.

"Yes, Sheriff?" She knew what he wanted. She'd have to answer for shooting Darrin.

"We'll need your statement."

Standard procedure. "Of course. I'll be right outside."

Before she could turn away, the sheriff added, "And, Ms. Blain, if you ever decide you want to go back into law enforcement, you have a job with the Lane County sheriff's department waiting for you."

Warmth and pleasure washed over her. Longing to be back on the job hit her with the impact of a gale-force wind coming off the Atlantic Ocean in winter. But as tempting as the offer was, she couldn't take it.

She couldn't be this close to Wyatt and Gabby and not be in their lives.

And she didn't know if she was brave enough to risk her heart again. Even for one handsome cowboy and an adorable little girl.

Bright and early the next morning, Jackie set her packed bags on the front porch of her aunt and uncle's house. Spencer plopped down on the landing and panted as if the trek from the bedroom to the front door had been a mile-long excursion. Uncle Carl had said he'd take her to Laramie after he finished his morning chores.

Her boss, James Trent, had called several times last night and again this morning, making sure she was okay and to let her know the jet would be waiting to take her back to Boston when she arrived at the airstrip.

She should be happy to return home, but she couldn't stop the niggling feeling that had kept her up all night. One that still plagued her today.

Warm sunlight caressed her face and touched the ranch, melting the snow the same way Wyatt and his daughter had melted the ice around Jackie's heart, leaving her feeling raw and tender. And so unhappy about leaving.

She didn't want to return to Boston. She'd fallen in love with a handsome cowboy and a little red-haired four-year-old princess. Saying goodbye to them would be the hardest thing she'd ever done, much harder than walking away from the Atkins sheriff's department.

But what else could she do?

She'd realized she wasn't brave enough to talk to Wyatt about her feelings. She couldn't risk being rejected by him. Yet she at least wanted a few minutes to say goodbye.

But after they'd returned to the ranch last night, he'd taken Gabby and disappeared inside the house with a quiet thank-you and good-night. What had she expected? For him to declare his undying love and beg her to stay?

Yes, her heart screamed.

But it hadn't happened. Not when she'd barged into

his life uninvited. He wanted his life to return to normal. A life that didn't include her.

She forced herself to breathe. She had a feeling it would be a long time before she forgot anything that had happened in the past few days. She wasn't sure she'd ever forget Wyatt.

Feeling antsy, Jackie longed to go for a run, to work out the tension in her limbs and her heart. But she'd dressed for the return flight to Boston. Comfortable stretch pants and a tank under a loose-fitting sweater. Her hair was caught up in a band, the weight of it pulling at her scalp, making her head ache. With a yank she pulled the tie away and let the curls fall haphazardly about her shoulders. Much better.

If only she could fix the ache in her heart as easily.

She sank to the top step and leaned back against the railing. The quiet peacefulness of the ranch soothed her soul. As vacations went, this one was a doozy. Best to get back to work and keep her nose to the grindstone for a while. The quicker she moved onto a new assignment, the better.

Spencer barked. His nails scraped on the wood as he stood.

Wyatt and Gabby came out of their house and walked across the drive toward them. Tall and broad shouldered in his jeans, chambray shirt and cowboy hat, Wyatt made Jackie sigh with longing. She forced herself to swallow back the yearning jamming her throat and fought against the tears burning her eyes.

Not good. Maybe she should have left already.

Love for this man and child filled her with a bittersweet joy. She was so thankful God had spared them both. That she'd had some part in keeping them safe. She knew it would take time for Wyatt to deal with all the ramifications of learning about Darrin being his brother and trying to kill him. He had decisions to make about the uranium mining. And he needed to make sure Gabby would feel safe and secure after being kidnapped.

But Jackie had no doubt Wyatt was up for the task.

She blinked to keep the tears at bay.

Halfway across the drive, Gabby broke into a run, her little legs pumping, her arms flailing. She wore jeans and a sweatshirt with Mickey Mouse on the front. Her red curls bounced with each footfall. She bounded up the steps and launched herself at Jackie.

Catching her around the waist, Jackie hugged her close. Tears filled her eyes. She couldn't help it. She was going to miss this little girl. Jackie met Wyatt's gaze. The tenderness there in his eyes almost undid her. She blinked again, feeling the wetness of tears on her lashes.

Spencer barked, demanding his share of attention. Releasing Jackie, Gabby threw her arms around the dog's neck.

"Why don't you take Spencer for a walk around the house?" Wyatt said, ruffling his daughter's hair.

Gabby jumped up. "Come on, Spencer. Let's go."

She bounded down the stairs, patting her leg as she went. Spencer scrambled after her. The two disappeared around the corner of the house as Gabby's laughter rose in the air. The happy sound pinched Jackie's heart.

"So you're all set to leave," Wyatt said, his gaze on her bags.

"Yes. All packed up and waiting for Uncle Carl," she murmured.

For a moment neither spoke. Anxious flurries stirred in her tummy. She hated goodbyes. They were always so painfully awkward.

"I thought about what you said, about confirming Gabby's paternity." Wyatt finally broke the silence. "I'm going to have a DNA test done."

"Oh, no," she exclaimed as guilt rushed in. She'd forgotten to tell him. "You don't have to. Gabby's yours."

"I know she's mine. She'll always be my little girl, but…"

Jackie jumped to her feet and took his hand. "No, I mean, she is your child. Boyd said he and Dina never…"

He sank to the stair, pulling Jackie down with him. "I'm glad to hear that. I guess. I really don't know how to feel or think or…" He shrugged. "Boyd might not be who Dina was referring to."

Jackie ached for Wyatt. So much had happened the past few days, revelations that would take time to wrap his mind around. She wished she could be here to help him process them. She tried to slip her hands from his, but he held on tight.

She stared at him with unspoken questions.

He stared back as if memorizing her face. "I'm so jumbled up inside right now."

"I understand. You've been through a great deal."

Intensity filled his expression. "But the one thing I'm not confused about is you."

Her heart jolted. "Me?"

"Yes. You. I don't want you to leave. I know I have no right to ask you to stay. But I need you. Gabby needs you."

His words were like arrows straight to her heart. "You're safe now. You don't need me."

"But I do. More than you could possibly know." He brought her hands to his lips and kissed her knuckles. "I love you, Jackie Blain. I want to spend the rest of my life with you. Even if that means following you to Boston."

Her pulse galloped away. Joy ballooned in her soul. "Really?"

The corners of his mouth tipped upward. "Yes, really."

"I love you, too." Her voice broke. Tears slipped unchecked down her cheeks. "I can't imagine anywhere on earth I'd rather be than here with you and Gabby. Here on the ranch. And I really want to be a sheriff's deputy again."

"Really?" He echoed her question.

She laughed with giddy elation. "Really."

He captured her lips and kissed her deeply, thoroughly.

The tinkling sound of a child's giggle broke them apart. Gabby and Spencer stood at the bottom of the stairs.

Jackie and Wyatt opened their arms. Gabby rushed up the stairs, wedged herself between them and grabbed each of their hands.

Filled to the brim with love, Jackie looked over Gabby's head to meet Wyatt's adoring gaze. Jackie had found the perfect place to belong. Wyatt leaned forward and kissed her again, cementing her happiness forever.

* * * * *

*If you enjoyed this story by Terri Reed,
be sure to look for SCENT OF DANGER,
part of the TEXAS K-9 UNIT continuity,
coming in May from Terri and
Love Inspired Suspense!*

Dear Reader,

I hope you enjoyed traveling to Wyoming with Jackie and meeting the cowboy who captured her heart. Single father Wyatt Monroe thought he'd never love again. That is, until pretty and feisty Jackie barged into his life, determined to keep him and his daughter safe.

I enjoyed writing Jackie and Wyatt's story. They were complex characters who were fun to write. The setting was a new one for me. I enjoyed learning about Wyoming and hope one day to see the state and the Snowy Range Mountains.

Coming next in May, look for *Scent of Danger,* book five of the TEXAS K-9 UNIT continuity series.

Until we meet again, God bless,

Questions for Discussion

1. What made you pick up this book to read? In what ways did it live up to your expectations?

2. In what ways were Jackie and Wyatt realistic characters? In what ways did their romance build believably?

3. If you read other books in the Protection Specialists series, then you met Jackie before. In what ways did she meet your expectations?

4. As Jackie and Wyatt worked together to solve the murder and uncover the reasons why he was a target, how did the suspense build?

5. What about the setting was clear and appealing? What did you like most about the setting?

6. Have you ever visited or lived on a working ranch? If so, can you describe that experience?

7. Wyatt thought he was an only child. How did learning he had a sibling affect him? Do you have siblings? What is your relationship like?

8. Jackie pressed Wyatt to find out the truth about Gabby's paternity. Do you agree that knowing one's DNA is important? If so, why? If not, why not?

9. Jackie tells Wyatt that whenever life seems random and chaotic, she uses scripture to remind herself

that God has a plan for her. Do you have a favorite scripture that you cling to?

10. The drilling of uranium is controversial. Share your opinions on the mining of this element.

11. Wyatt had to come to terms with the lies his father told him about his mother. Do you have an experience to share where you realized someone had lied to you about another person?

12. Jackie thought her life was fulfilled by being a part of a team, but she realized she wanted to be a part of a family. In what ways does being part of a family fulfill you?

13. Did you notice the scripture in the beginning of the book? What do you think God means by these words? What application does the scripture have to your life?

14. How did the author's use of language/writing style make this an enjoyable read?

15. What will be your most vivid memories of this book? What lessons about life, love and faith did you learn from this story?

REQUEST YOUR FREE BOOKS!

2 FREE RIVETING INSPIRATIONAL NOVELS
PLUS 2 FREE MYSTERY GIFTS

Love Inspired®
SUSPENSE

YES! Please send me 2 FREE Love Inspired® Suspense novels and my 2 FREE mystery gifts (gifts are worth about $10). After receiving them, if I don't wish to receive any more books, I can return the shipping statement marked "cancel." If I don't cancel, I will receive 4 brand-new novels every month and be billed just $4.49 per book in the U.S. or $4.99 per book in Canada. That's a savings of at least 22% off the cover price. It's quite a bargain! Shipping and handling is just 50¢ per book in the U.S. and 75¢ per book in Canada.* I understand that accepting the 2 free books and gifts places me under no obligation to buy anything. I can always return a shipment and cancel at any time. Even if I never buy another book, the two free books and gifts are mine to keep forever.

123/323 IDN FVWV

Name _____ (PLEASE PRINT) _____

Address _____ Apt. # _____

City _____ State/Prov. _____ Zip/Postal Code _____

Signature (if under 18, a parent or guardian must sign)

Mail to the **Harlequin® Reader Service:**
IN U.S.A.: P.O. Box 1867, Buffalo, NY 14240-1867
IN CANADA: P.O. Box 609, Fort Erie, Ontario L2A 5X3

**Are you a subscriber to Love Inspired Suspense
and want to receive the larger-print edition?
Call 1-800-873-8635 or visit www.ReaderService.com.**

* Terms and prices subject to change without notice. Prices do not include applicable taxes. Sales tax applicable in N.Y. Canadian residents will be charged applicable taxes. Offer not valid in Quebec. This offer is limited to one order per household. Not valid for current subscribers to Love Inspired Suspense books. All orders subject to credit approval. Credit or debit balances in a customer's account(s) may be offset by any other outstanding balance owed by or to the customer. Please allow 4 to 6 weeks for delivery. Offer available while quantities last.

Your Privacy—The Harlequin® Reader Service is committed to protecting your privacy. Our Privacy Policy is available online at www.ReaderService.com or upon request from the Harlequin Reader Service.

We make a portion of our mailing list available to reputable third parties that offer products we believe may interest you. If you prefer that we not exchange your name with third parties, or if you wish to clarify or modify your communication preferences, please visit us at www.ReaderService.com/consumerchoice or write to us at Harlequin Reader Service Preference Service, P.O. Box 9062, Buffalo, NY 14269. Include your complete name and address.

LIS13

SPECIAL EXCERPT FROM

Love Inspired.
SUSPENSE

*Nicolette Johnson is pregnant and on a crime
syndicate's hit list.*

*Read on for a preview of the next book in the exciting
TEXAS K-9 UNIT series, EXPLOSIVE SECRETS
by Valerie Hansen.*

Nicolette Johnson was about to leave for her night shift job
as a short-order cook at the Highway Twenty Truck Stop
when her cell phone rang.

She slipped it out of her jeans pocket and hesitated while
she listened to it playing "The Yellow Rose of Texas." Most
of her recent callers had been nosy reporters or curious
neighbors wanting to ask what she knew about her cousin
Arianna Munson's recent murder.

"That would be *nothing,* just like I told the police," she
muttered. Still, she gave in and answered. "Hello?"

"Hello, Nicki, darlin'."

The slow, deep drawl was dripping with menace, sending
chills up her spine. "Who is this?"

"Never mind who I am. You need to stop holding out on
us," the man warned. "Remember, we know where you live."

Nicki swallowed past the lump in her throat. "I don't
know what you're talking about. Leave me alone."

"That's not going to happen, lady. That idiot Murke blew
it the other night, but we can still get to you, just like we got
to your cousin. We eliminated her and we can do the same
to you. If you think you can run or hide, just ask the Sagebrush cops what happened to one of their wives a few years

back." He chortled again then shouted, *"Boom!"*

Nicki immediately ended the call. Many of the specifics of the man's threats had already become a confusing muddle but one fact stood out. The way he had barked "boom" left no doubt that she was dealing with a deadly enemy.

Shaking, Nicki managed to punch in the phone number from the business card the police officers had left with her a few days earlier. She held her breath and counted the number of rings while she waited for them to answer.

"Sagebrush Police and Sheriff. How may I help you?" a friendly sounding woman asked.

Nicki had intended to report the scary warning calmly and with little emotion. When she heard the dispatcher's voice, however, she blurted, "I need help. Somebody just threatened to blow me up!"

Can K-9 officer Jackson Worth and his
bomb-sniffing dog, Titan, keep Nicki safe?
Pick up EXPLOSIVE SECRETS by Valerie Hansen,
available April 2013 from Love Inspired Suspense.

LISEXP0313

Love Inspired

SUSPENSE

RIVETING INSPIRATIONAL ROMANCE

A mafia boss wants Kate Townsend to stop asking questions...

His tactic? Send one of his thugs to intimidate her at gunpoint. FBI Agent Logan Quail knows too well what violence Bernardo Salvatore is capable of, and he doesn't hesitate to intervene...blowing his cover in the process. He wasn't able to save his fiancé. But this time, he'll make darn sure this foolhardy little filly doesn't get herself killed trying to prove her father was murdered. Now, Logan and Kate must work together, each overcoming their separate grief, to bring down a ruthless syndicate. And maybe, just maybe, find some peace through the healing power of love.

UNDERCOVER COWBOY

by

LAURA SCOTT

LIS44534